WAR
AND MILLIE
McGONIGLE

WAR
AND MILLIE
McGONIGLE

KAREN CUSHMAN

A YEARLING BOOK

Text copyright © 2021 by Karen Cushman
Cover art copyright © 2021 by Izzy Burton

All rights reserved. Published in the United States by Yearling, an imprint of Random House Children's Books, a division of Penguin Random House LLC, New York. Originally published in hardcover in the United States by Alfred A. Knopf, an imprint of Random House Children's Books, a division of Penguin Random House LLC, New York, in 2021.

Yearling and the jumping horse design are registered trademarks of Penguin Random House LLC.

Visit us on the Web! rhcbooks.com

Educators and librarians, for a variety of teaching tools, visit us at RHTeachersLibrarians.com

Library of Congress Cataloging-in-Publication Data is available upon request.
ISBN 978-1-9848-5010-2 (trade) — ISBN 978-1-9848-5011-9 (lib. bdg.) —
ISBN 978-1-9848-5012-6 (ebook) — ISBN 978-1-9848-5013-3 (pbk.)

Printed in the United States of America
10 9 8 7 6 5 4 3 2 1
First Yearling Edition 2022

*For Frances and Maxine, the Segal girls of San Diego—
and with thanks to Philip, for sharing his memories
and for, well, everything*

THIS WAS A PEOPLE'S WAR,
AND EVERYONE WAS IN IT.

———

—Colonel Oveta Culp Hobby,
inscribed on the World War II Memorial,
Washington, D.C.

SEPTEMBER 20, 1941
SATURDAY

George lifted the slimy creature to his mouth and bit it right between the eyes. I had seen him and the other Portuguese octopus fishermen do that a hundred times, but it still made me shudder. "Doesn't that taste muddy and disgusting?"

"Nah," he said, wiping his mouth on his sleeve. "Only salty. I told you, this way he don't die but only sleeps, stays fresh 'til he's cooked."

George threw the octopus into a bucket and slid over to another hole in the mud. He filled a turkey baster from a grimy Clorox bottle and squirted the bleach into the hole. In a minute another octopus slithered to the surface to avoid the bleach. George grabbed it, pulled it out, and bit it. "You want? Makes good stew."

Another shudder ran up my back, and I shook my head. I'd as soon eat sand-flea soup or mud-snail chowder! I'll take my fish from a can, thank you, mixed with mayo and chopped onion. Black olives, maybe. Anyway, the McGonigles' money troubles, bad as they were, did not require us to eat octopus stew. Not yet, anyway.

I pulled my Book of Dead Things from the waistband of my shorts.

The octopuses in the bucket weren't exactly dead, but close enough, I decided, to add to the book. Squatting down, I examined them closely: squishy and grayish with yellow splotches, many legs, bright blue eyes on . . . "Hey, George, octopuses have blue eyes!"

He wiped his face with his wet and muddy hands, leaving his face wet and muddy. "Nah, those fake eyes." He pulled another from its hole. "Their real eyes up here, see."

I looked. Indeed the octopus's real eyes were higher on its head. Dark and kind of sad. And George bit it right between them.

I sketched an octopus as best I could, not being any kind of artist. My drawing looked like a blob of nothing, which is pretty much what the octopuses looked like but with bright blue fake eyes.

Tucking my book away, I walked on. Above me the September sun was bright and warm. In San Diego it was almost always bright and warm. People called it paradise, but often I've longed for a dreary day—heavy dark clouds, wind whistling over the water, rain tapping on the roof and falling *plop plop plop,* leaving little pockmarks on the sand. Mama snorts when I say this and calls me a romantic. I don't think it's meant as a compliment.

Except for the fishermen, I was alone on the beach. Summer visitors were mostly gone. Mission Beach is a spit of land two blocks wide and two miles long, with the ocean on one side and the bay on the other. Likely there were sunbathers and sand-castle builders over on the ocean side, but here on the bay it was quiet, with a scattering of cottages—some new, some shabby, all small—and few people to bother me. That was the way I liked it. I had tides to watch and dead things to find.

I sat myself on the end of the Lempkes' dock, one of several wooden docks that reached out as if trying to touch the tiny island in the middle of the bay. The tide was out, and the mudflats, speckled with eelgrass, were alive with fiddler crabs, flies, and sand fleas. Here and there, a boat marooned in the mud squeaked and scraped, awaiting the high tides that would float it once again. Twice a day, every day, the tide came in and went out. Pop said the changing tides were caused by gravitational forces related to the sun and the moon. I didn't understand how it worked, but each day I saw the waters of the bay recede and leave behind an expanse of mud and sand, and then return blue and deep. I could count on it. Every day the same.

I lay back on the warm boards of the dock, scratched the flea bites on my leg, and sniffed deeply of the rich, salty, fishy smell of the mud. Gulls screeched like rusty hinges as they soared above me, and flocks of curlews and sandpipers pecked for bugs for breakfast. There was plenty of life on the bay but a peaceful stillness, too, that comforted me when I needed comforting.

A brown pelican came to a clumsy landing on the mud and shook water from its feathers. "What're you doing here?" I asked. The bird studied me closely with its dark, beady eyes but said nothing.

"Have you come to try and cheer me up, too? Everyone wants me to cheer up, but I refuse. Know why?" I sat up and glared at the bird. "The world's full of war and death. That's why. Hitler's gobbling up one country after another, and I'm afraid he'll come here next. My pop can't find a job, Mama's crabby, and Lily is sick all the time. What's there to be cheery about?" I took a deep breath and let it out with a *whoof*. "Want to hear more?"

The bird made loud clacking sounds with its enormous beak but still said nothing, just yawned a huge yawn and ruffled its feathers. Then it hopped awkwardly down the beach, flapping its mighty wings before soaring into the air, growing smaller and smaller until it disappeared. That's what I get for trying to have a serious discussion with a pelican. Stupid bird.

I pulled out my Book of Dead Things again. Next to the octopus blob, I drew what else I'd found this morning—six sand dollars stuck together with tar, a faintly orange ghost shrimp, and a sand crab no bigger than my thumb. I was trying to capture what exactly marked them as dead: the lifeless droop of the shrimp's pincers, the emptiness in the eyes of the crab. Where were they now? Why did they die and not some other shrimp or crab? Why did Gram die?

She did die. In July. On my birthday, of all days. It was so wrong and unfair. We had all gone to a matinee of the new Bob Hope comedy, *Caught in the Draft*, to celebrate my birthday. There were awful newsreels about the war in Europe and the movie was about soldiers and danger and shooting, and I started to think again about war and death.

What a world. Even Bob Hope movies left me worried and scared.

When we got home, I was gloomier than usual. Mama told me to get out until I was in a better mood, so Gram and I took a walk along the bay.

Still grumbling, I picked up stones and bombarded the water, the seagulls, the piers and docks we passed.

Gram grabbed my hand and held it still. "Where has my Millie gone, my merry squirt, my grumbly but funny dance partner and poker buddy? She had the biggest laugh. Anyone who heard it had to laugh, too. I don't hear that laugh anymore."

"Sorry, Gram, but this is how I am now. Better get used to glum and scared."

Gram shook her head. "Bah, you've just taken on the world's troubles sooner than a young person should have to. Too sensitive and smart for your own good, if you ask me. Now you're no longer a merry squirt, you're a gloomy squirt. And a gloomy squirt, dear Millie, can be a pain in the backsi—um, neck."

I hid a smile at that before responding. "Why shouldn't I be gloomy? You know what's happening in the world. Hitler marching with tanks and planes and goose-stepping Nazis. Radios and newspapers and newsreels at the movies shouting about war and bombs, ruined cities, dead soldiers, loss and pain. How can I not think about that? And how can I not be gloomy about it?"

"I know. Terrible things are happening, but it's not all tragedy and death." She dropped my hand and gestured vigorously around, the loose skin on her arm moving like little waves on the bay. "Look, Millie, at this amazing place you live in. The sun and the warm breezes, the sea and the sky, the birds in the air, and the marvels of life in the sea. They can bring you joy. Remember them. Treasure them. Don't let them be lost in your gloom."

I would not be comforted. "But they die, the birds and the fish. I see them dead on the beach all the time. And what if Nazi bombs destroy the beach and the bay and everything in it?" I drew in a deep breath.

She put her arm around my shoulders. "Ah, Millie, of course you're worried, but life's not hopeless. We can do something about what worries and scares us. That's why I march, pass out flyers, circulate petitions." She gave my shoulders a squeeze. "And I'm not the only one. Despite the horror, people care, work together for a better world, and bravely fight back. There's good, even in wartime—remember that."

"What do you mean?" My voice got tight and screechy. And loud. "What's good about war and death?"

Gram pulled a package wrapped in *Happy Birthday* paper and a green ribbon out of the pocket of her jacket. She made me unwrap it right there. Inside was a bright yellow notebook and a purple pen. "I thought you might like to keep a diary," she said, "but now I have a better idea. Use this to remember the good things in this world, the things you care about. Family and friends, sunrises and sunsets, the birds in the air and the fish in the bay. Things that seem lost or dead—keep them alive and safe in your book. Write. Draw pictures. Whatever is lost stays alive if we remember it."

I was happy with the notebook but unsure about Gram's idea. Did she really mean I should be drawing pictures of dead things? It was too late to keep *them* safe. Did she mean keep *us* safe? It was confusing. Still, I thanked her and hugged her before we went back home.

After the twelve candles had been blown out, twelve kisses given, and the cake eaten, Gram had gone home. As she left, she gestured to the notebook and said, "Don't let yourself forget, Millie." It was the last thing she ever said to me.

At the cemetery, I threw rocks at the gravestones and refused to watch her being put into the ground. That was when I ripped the cheery yellow cover into a million pieces and turned the notebook into *The Book of Dead Things, Mission Beach, San Diego, California, 1941.*

SEPTEMBER 21, 1941
SUNDAY

I drew several dead clams in my book and closed it with a slam. With my bare feet, I wrote **MCGONIGLE** in the muddy ground, embellished with whorls and squiggles. I considered it signing my work like artists and authors do.

We McGonigles do not go to church. Not, Gram used to say, until the pope got married so he'd know what life was really like. But I had my own rituals—drawing things lost or dead in my notebook like Gram told me to and signing my name in the mud. The same things in the same way every day. When I don't, I feel itchy and uncomfortable.

The mud of the flats felt soft and cool on my bare feet. I wiggled them so the muck squidged between my toes. Marching in place, I sank lower and lower until I was in mud well past my ankles. Then I wiggled and wriggled my legs until the mud gave me up, and I turned for home.

On Bayside Walk, I passed the few houses, cottages, and downright shacks that straggled along the bay side of Mission Beach. I knew most everyone there, though not everyone wanted to be known, which was okay with me. I am not the chatty-with-the-neighbors sort.

I nodded to Myrtle Henry, who was sunbathing in her nightgown, and snorted as I passed the Sweeneys'. The only big tree in South Mission, a giant pine, grew in the Sweeneys' yard. Herman Sweeney tried to climb to the top one New Year's Eve, but he fell off. People say he only survived because he was drunk and relaxed, but Herman says no, he was saved by an angel. He's okay now, but his nose is squashed like a potato.

Behind me sounded the *beep beep* of a horn and the squeaking tires of a bike. I knew that sound—Dicky Fribble, my archenemy. Once I saw him get beaten up near the roller coaster at the amusement center. Boys often got roughed up there, and that time it was Icky. They swung on him and pushed him around. He was crying when they left. Icky must have seen me because we've been archenemies ever since, although I never told anyone what I saw. Superman had Lex Luthor; Captain America had the Red Skull; I had Dicky Fribble.

"Greetings and salutations, Mil-bert," Dicky said, slowing down as he passed. "My, but you're dirty. You should have done the world a favor and smeared that mud all over your ugly face."

"Hello, Icky. Drop dead," I said, and strode off, my legs dark and gooey.

"Hey, Millie!" Ralphie Rigoletto ran up behind me, pulling his red Radio Flyer wagon. "Come meet my new turtle. I won him at a carnival, and I want him to meet everyone."

There, in the wagon, bouncing in an inch of water, was a little turtle, its shell painted yellow with a tiny green palm tree. "His name is Pepperoni."

"Why Pepperoni?"

"Because I love pepperoni," Ralphie said. "You can pet him for a penny."

"That's a penny more than I have."

"Then I'll give you one free pet." I reached out to touch Pepperoni's painted back, and he pulled his head in.

"He doesn't know you. Maybe he's scared," Ralphie said. "Turtles do that when they're scared."

I waved Ralphie and Pepperoni on to meet the rest of the neighbors and headed toward home, a small cottage perched near the south end of Mission Beach. We could often hear waves crashing on the ocean beach to the west, but the cottage faced the gentler activity of the bay.

"Millie, is that you?" Mama called as I entered.

Who else? "I saw Pop with Lily and Pete on their way to the amusement center, so I guess it must be me." *Or were you expecting Cary Grant to come and take you away from your ungrateful family and sweep you off to Hollywood?* The drying mud on my legs itched, so I threw myself down on a kitchen chair and began scratching it off with a fork.

"Millie, if you can't act like a lady, at least try to act like a human being." Mama took a slurp of her coffee. "I sent your father and the little ones out so we could talk," she said.

Uh-oh. Danger. Mama never sat me down to talk. My skin prickled. "Is it bad war news? Is somebody sick? Or dead?" Dead! I patted the Book of Dead Things in my pocket.

"Calm down, Nervous Nelly," Mama said. "It's nothing like that." She lit a cigarette and blew a great puff of smoke into the air. "But some big changes are coming for us."

I hated changes. I wanted a world I could count on. I fought a sudden urge to write **MCGONIGLE** in the mud.

"It's about Gram's cousin Edna," Mama said. "She was in some sort of trouble back in Milwaukee, which is how she landed on Gram's doorstep. But now Gram is gone"— tears glittered in Mama's eyes—"and Edna can't be left alone. Last week she walked out of the Piggly Wiggly with a ham tucked under her jacket." Mama waved her cigarette around. "And yesterday she set the stove on fire! So we'll have to give up Gram's apartment, and Edna will come here and live with us."

"Mama, you can't mean it! We're already too crowded. Where will she sleep, and—" I knew. There were only two bedrooms in the cottage, and sure as shootin', Cousin Edna wouldn't be bunking with my parents.

"She'll move in with Lily and you, and Pete will use the sofa."

"But—"

"I know. I know what you're going to say. She has no sense. She loses her glasses and leaves her false teeth lying around. She smells of too much perfume, hair dye, and her stomach trouble."

Stomach trouble, Mama called it. Truth is, Edna was a stink machine, burping and hiccuping and passing gas. Hook her up and she could power all the stoves in San Diego!

"Edna is family," Mama continued, "and we'll be there

for her. That's what my mother would have wanted." She blinked hard a few times. "And that's it."

"Can't we pay someone to live with her? Or build an extra room on our house, like a—"

"And where do we get the money for that? We lost the store in the Depression, your dad can't find work, and I scrimp and save to feed us all on less than eight dollars a week."

"But—"

"But nothing." Mama stubbed her cigarette out in a saucer and wiped her eyes. "This is a family, not a democracy."

As if that hadn't been obvious every day of my life. "But I won't speak to her until the day I die," I shouted as I stomped into the bedroom and slammed the door. I stuck my head out the window and took a deep breath. Some people said the mudflats stink. It could be pretty strong at times, but to me it was the smell of home.

Airplanes roared overhead, three of them, looping and diving. My belly cramped. No doubt a training mission from the naval training base in Point Loma, but the sound was ominous. These planes could just as well be Nazis coming from Germany to bomb Mission Beach. Folks said it was only a matter of time before they came here, bringing war with them. And they expected me to cheer up. Phooey to that.

After dinner, as I was getting ready for bed, I heard Mama and Pop outside. Mama was almost shouting. This might not seem such a big deal to most people, but my mother graduated from the School of No Arguing or Whining, where she studied Never Raise Your Voice and Act Like a Lady.

"We're not going to keep my mother's radio, Martin," Mama was saying. "I'll sell it with her other things to Big Ernie's Second Hand and buy what we need: shoes for Lily and Pete, a warm jacket for Millie, a new ribbon for my old hat. We can pay the electric bill and eat something every once in a while that's not spaghetti or a fish you caught. A radio is just a frill."

"A radio is not a frill. Things are happening in the world, things we need to know about. And our children should—"

"I don't want to know, and the children don't need to be frightened."

"There's a war on, Lois."

"Not here."

"Not yet."

Pop would win the argument, I knew. I myself was of two minds about a radio. On one hand, I could listen to *The Aldrich Family* as I had at Gram's. Henry was a teenager and I would turn thirteen next summer, so I needed to know all I could about being a teenager. But a radio would bring war news right into the house. The war was in Europe, thousands of miles away, in places I couldn't spell, and I wanted it to stay there.

What with sickly Lily getting all the attention, and smelly Edna moving in, and no money, and the war coming closer and closer, I felt the dread that was all too familiar. I wished I could be like Ralphie's turtle and just pull my head in, but instead I closed my eyes and burrowed into my pillow.

War! War! War! Would America be attacked? What if

bombs killed us all? Gee whiz, I wasn't even thirteen yet. Was this all the life I'd get? Never have a date or a kiss or grow breasts? Christopher Columbus!

That night I dreamed of hundreds of enemy airplanes roaring by, but it turned out to be Pop snoring. Good gravy!

SEPTEMBER 28, 1941
SUNDAY

Cousin Edna moved in with her greasy green face cream, pink flannel nightgown, and Jungle Gardenia perfume. Edna thought she smelled like a tropical princess, but the perfume definitely had a hint of funeral parlor.

Pete was only five and a half, so it was a great adventure to sleep in the living room. He wore his Lone Ranger pajamas and called the couch his bunk.

Lily got the twin bed to herself, of course. That left the big bed for me to share with Cousin Edna. I confronted Mama: "Why me? I'm the oldest. Don't you think I should have first choice of bed?" *Let me win, Mama. This time, let me win.*

But Mama said, "You know Lily is delicate and needs her rest. Edna is a fidgety sleeper, so it has to be you."

Lily rolled and stretched as she delighted in her own bed. "You could have a bed to yourself if you were special like me." She coughed a little cough and smiled. "But you're not. Too bad for you, Millie." Lily had some kind of lung trouble and used it to get her way, and Mama let her. I wished I were an only child, except I'd miss Pete. Maybe he could come and visit me sometimes.

I stormed out of the room, and who could blame me? Lily always came first. Lily, the favorite child, who was seven but babyish. Lily, who was sickly and needed coddling. Lily, who was too weak to sweep the floor or take out the garbage. Lily, who still slept with a doll that had a new name every week because Lily couldn't decide on one. This week she called it Pepsi. Who the heck names a doll Pepsi? Only cutie-pie Lily, who looked like the movie star Shirley Temple with her corkscrew curls and dimples. Lily was a pill and so was Shirley Temple. I was tempted to sprinkle some sticker-bush thorns in that precious bed she gets all to herself, but I'd probably get blamed. So unfair.

I could tell by the fog of gardenia fumes that Edna was home. In the kitchen Pop was struggling to get Pete out of his wet bathing suit while Mama slammed pots around and grumbled about trying to stretch one box of Kraft macaroni and cheese with enough plain noodles to feed six people. And the radio blared about the war, about Nazi submarines sinking British ships, and the massacre of thousands of Jews someplace in Russia. It was a nightmare.

Pushing aside the coats in the front closet, I crawled in with an apple, looking for some privacy, five minutes away from my family and the radio.

Someone knocked on the closet door. Five minutes. I couldn't even have five minutes' peace. "What?"

"Cousin Edna," said Pete, "has a date and she can't find her teeth. Mama's making dinner and Pop is washing Lily's hair, so I'm looking for the teeth. I need you to help me."

A date? Who would date Edna? She must be over forty! Curious, I joined the hunt. Pete searched under the sofa, behind the rocking chair, under the rug. I dug through the bedroom closet while Edna turned out dresser drawers, muttering as she searched. Finally she dropped onto the bed. "*Mein Gott,* what will I do? *Mein Gott.*" Irish Cousin Edna had once dated a German butcher, who left her with a smattering of German words and a fondness for sauerkraut. "I can't go out with no teeth!"

I looked closely at Edna. I had pledged never to speak to her again, but someone had to tell her. "Good gravy, Edna, your teeth are in your mouth!"

Edna smacked her head. "My *glasses*! I meant my *glasses* are lost."

We undertook another search and Pete found Edna's glasses stuck in her copy of *Photoplay* magazine. Edna clapped her hands. "Yes, I remember now. I was reading about Clark Gable! Such a good-looking man. I do like a man with a mustache." She put her glasses on. "Now I can see to make myself beautiful."

"Good luck," I muttered, and I pinched the *Photoplay* magazine to read later. Clark Gable. Yowza!

Edna brushed her hair down and pinned a mat of black fur in the back. It looked creepy and weird. "What's that?" I asked.

"It's a rat," said Edna, her mouth full of bobby pins.

"A rat?"

The very word drew Pete over. "A rat?" he echoed. "Where? Can I see? Can I have it?"

Rolling her hair up over the rat, Edna said, "A rat is

padding to give my hairstyle fullness and body, so the magazines say." She stabbed the rat with bobby pins. "See? I look like a movie star."

"It looks like you have a sausage on the back of your head," said Pete.

"Pooh," said Edna. "It's very stylish. Betty Grable, watch out! Edna Duffy's coming!" She coated her lips with lipstick, smacked them together, and checked to make sure her teeth had not turned red.

With a final spray of perfume, Edna proclaimed herself ready. She plunked her hat on her head, and calling "*Auf Wiedersehen,* goodbye" and blowing kisses, she left.

I opened the windows wide.

Pete pulled on my sleeve. "Who would take Edna on a date?" he whispered.

"Maybe the Three Stooges?" I said. And I went *nyuk-nyuk-nyuk* and rubbed his head with my knuckles. Pete was my favorite McGonigle. He was funny and curious and told the truth.

Like Gram.

Gram always said I was her special girl, her *macushla,* her sweetheart. It was what her own grandmother had called her. Mama didn't really want me once she had Lily to coddle, and Pop was too busy looking for work or flipping burgers at the Shack when they had need of him. Busy as she was, Gram always had time for me. We talked about things like why Lily was such a pill (Gram disagreed but she listened) and why I couldn't quit school and get a job on a fishing boat (she had no good reason, in my opinion), but still we had fun.

Gram and I liked the same things. Eggs scrambled, not

fried. Big rainstorms. "Why did the chicken cross the road?" jokes. Words that feel good in the mouth like *chortle* and *muffin* and *fling*. We thought Frank Sinatra was too skinny and Groucho Marx the funniest Marx brother, but we liked Harpo best.

She taught me to dance the Charleston, like she did when she was young. We'd bend our knees and swing our arms, and our skirts flew. "*Dance-mad Tillie,* they used to call me," she said. "They'd holler *hotsy-totsy* and *You're the bee's knees,* and I'd dance, dance, dance." They obviously spoke a different language then.

She used to brush my scraggly, sun-bleached hair with her silver brush, a hundred strokes to make it shine, though it never did, and sing "When Irish Eyes Are Smiling." It was her favorite song after "Down on the Picket Line" and "Which Side Are You On?"

Sometimes we played poker with her neighbor Barney, who was at least a hundred. Gram loved poker, but I'd get grumpy when I lost. And I always lost. She said it would be dishonest to let me win, but I think she just liked winning herself so much. She'd rub her hands together with glee and scoop up all the matches in the pot. There's no dancing or games on Bayside Walk these days. And no Gram.

When I was scared, Gram would make me weak tea and toast and let me sleep in her bed. She said she'd always be here to keep me safe. But she isn't. Whose special girl was I now?

SEPTEMBER 30, 1941
TUESDAY

Instead of me having the dreamboat Mr. Lester for sixth grade, Uncle Sam got him. I got stuck with the world's oldest teacher, Mrs. Gillicuddy, who retired from being retired to come and torture us.

Today for current events she made us watch a filmstrip about the war in Europe. Planes cut through the sky like black birds. Sirens wailed, bombs whistled, and then *boom, boom, boom!* All you could see was flames and rubble as buildings exploded and whole streets disappeared in fire. People ran in panic as soldiers pulled bodies out of the wreckage and carried stretcher after stretcher of the dead. My heart pounded and I had to close my eyes a lot of the time.

There was a little girl, no older than Pete, carrying a stuffed bunny. The bunny's long ears flopped as the girl ran. There were flashes of light and then darkness. What happened to her, I don't know. I sat frozen with fear. Who could do such awful things to little children? It should even be against the law to make us watch it, but sadly no one came to arrest Mrs. Gillicuddy.

I thought about that film all the way home. What happens when a bomb hits you? Do you explode? Burst into flames? Or melt like ice cream the way the bad witch in *The Wizard of Oz* did?

Once home, I tried to hide in the closet to think and read, but Mama said I had to come out and help her or she'd drag me out by my earlobes. I'm nothing but unpaid labor around here. There oughta be a law.

Mama and I made meatballs for dinner. Actually they were more like rice and breadcrumb balls with a tiny bit of meat in them. Mama learned lots of food-stretching tricks during the Depression, and we had to eat the results. I patted the mixture between my palms and remembered George handling the octopus. "How poor does someone have to be to eat octopus?"

"It's not a matter of poor, Millie. Don't be snooty. Octopus is just another kind of fish. Some people think it's a delicacy."

"Have you ever eaten it?"

She nodded. "It's tasty, if a bit chewy. I don't cook it for us because your pop doesn't like it."

"Well, then, I wish he didn't like perch." I kept rolling meatballs. "I feel sorry for octopuses. I watch them scramble out of their holes in the mud, thinking they're escaping the bleach, only to be caught by something worse—George and a stewpot." I shivered. "Is that what the world is like now— only war and death and winding up in a stew?"

"For heaven's sake, Millie, that's enough. You've gotten so gloomy and overdramatic lately. And make those meatballs smaller."

Of course Mama didn't understand me. Most of the time she didn't even hear me. I felt like Joe Btfsplk—the sad little guy from the *Li'l Abner* comic strip with the permanent rain cloud over his head.

Pop was home for dinner, not temping at the Burger Shack, Edna and her Jungle Gardenia were out on a date again, and we had meatballs and spaghetti instead of fish. It would have been a not-so-bad day except for school and the awful filmstrip. After that, of course, I had no appetite, though I thought I'd better nibble on a meatball or two to keep my strength up.

"So how are my fine children this fine evening?" Pop asked, tomato sauce on his chin. "Lily, Millie, got anything to share? You guys in college yet? What's taking you so long?" No one laughed. There was only the noise of spaghetti slurping.

He had asked Lily the favorite first, I noticed. Like always. But it was okay. I didn't want to even think about school.

Pop pointed at Lily with his fork. "Come on, Lil, tell us, how's second grade?"

"I want to go to school, too," Pete interrupted. "Why can't I? I have things to learn."

Pop's mouth was full of meatball, so Mama said, "The school here at the beach doesn't have a kindergarten yet, but next year you'll be in first grade, complaining about school like your sisters."

Pop wiped his sticky red chin with his napkin and nodded in agreement.

"Next year." Pete huffed. "It's always next year or next week or next something. Never today." He sucked in a string of spaghetti. "What if there is something I need to know right away but I don't know it because of no school? What if that ruined my whole life? How would you feel?" He dropped his head onto the table in misery and—*ow!*— got spaghetti sauce in his eyes. Then there was wailing until Mama mopped him up.

Lily announced, "I got an A in arithmetic today, and I didn't wheeze once." Today's boast from Lily. What a pill!

Pop nodded. "Well done, Lil."

"And I'm going to call my doll Arithmetic."

"Great name for a doll. And you, Millie?"

I frowned and took a bite of meatball before answering. "School is . . . school. I have to wear skirts and shoes and sit inside all day, and I can't even see the bay. Mrs. Gillicuddy is awful, sixth grade is boring, and Florence is not there anymore." Florence was my best friend. She had moved away when her dad joined the army.

Mine was a split classroom. Half were immature little fifth-graders and the rest were boys, except for stuck-up Felicity Kendell, who wore tight, fuzzy sweaters and hung out with a bunch of older kids from the junior high. "There's no one I even talk to except Dicky Fribble when I have to, and I hate Dicky Fribble."

"Who doesn't?" said Pete.

"Give it time," said Pop. "You may be surprised. He could turn out to be your best friend." He chuckled at the very idea.

"Or maybe," I said as I chewed, "Hitler will drop a bomb on us and it won't matter anyway."

Mama shouted, "Millie!"

Lily squealed, "Bomb?" and began to cry.

Pete pulled his cap guns from the holster around his waist and fired off a few rounds—*Bang! Bang! Bang!* "Take that, Hitler!" Smoke and the sulfurous smell of the caps filled the air.

That did it. Lily was scared quiet and I didn't have to talk about school anymore. Mission accomplished.

The front door swung open and slammed against the wall. Edna dropped onto the sofa with a shuddering sigh. "My date didn't show up, the louse."

"Which Stooge was it?" asked Pete.

"Quiet, Pete," said Pop.

"No Stooge," Edna said, "but Harold. Stupid old Harold. I should have said yes to Leonard, who is boring but at least shows up."

Mama changed the subject. "More meatballs, Martin?" she asked Pop, passing him the bowl. "And, Edna, we'll talk more about these dates of yours later."

Getting ready for bed, Edna hogged the bathroom while she pinned her dyed black hair in little snails all over her head. Lily and I sat on the edge of the bathtub and watched her. "Do you like living with us?" Lily asked.

"I don't know yet," Edna said through the bobby pins held in her teeth. "I miss Tillie. She was funny and nice and hardly ever angry with me when I did dumb things."

Gram. I missed her, too, and I wanted her back. I wanted her here and safe. All of us, here and safe. I patted the book in my pocket.

Edna finished with her hair, and then she couldn't find her glasses again. Lily found them in the refrigerator.

"Is Cousin Edna crazy?" Lily asked me in a whisper as we brushed our teeth.

I spit before answering. "Mama says no. Cousin Edna just does stupid stuff sometimes, she forgets things, and she gets confused. That's why we inherited her now that Gram is gone."

Lily spit. "Tell me a story about Gram. I'm already forgetting her."

"Don't bother me. You remember her fine."

"*Nyah-ah*. Tell me or I'll wheeze and Mama will worry."

"Okay, okay. You're such a pill, Lily." I took an irritated breath. "So, once upon a time there was an old lady who was very little—"

"Little as me?"

"Don't be silly—little for a grown-up, but smart and tough, with the curliest hair you ever saw and funny little glasses she perched on the end of her nose. She worked at the public library downtown and every lunchtime went to the zoo, where she fed bread to the chickens, even though you're not supposed to." I could feel my eyes prickle.

"Tell me more," Lily said.

"Well, this old lady liked laughing, dancing, and sunshine. She had a crush on President Roosevelt, brought strangers home for supper, and always had a petition to right some wrong that she'd try and get people to sign. Every Sunday she came to visit her grandchildren, even though it took an hour on the bus, and she—"

"That's enough," said Lily. "I remember now."

And she died, I finished to myself. *She died.*

Did Gram know she was dying when it happened? Was

she afraid? Where was she now? Was she happy? Did they have poker in heaven? And petitions? And hungry chickens?

In the bedroom Cousin Edna was asleep, snoring softly, her teeth in a glass by the bed. Why was Gram gone and Cousin Edna still here?

OCTOBER 5, 1941
SUNDAY

The radio was on, of course, with news that a bomber on a training mission from the navy base in Point Loma had plunged in a spin into San Diego Bay, killing the fliers. Ensign G. A. Jungjohann, who was the pilot, and Machinist Mate J. J. Brewer, the announcer said. Knowing their names made them real. What were they like? Did they have families or girlfriends? Could they jitterbug?

"I'm going for a walk," I called to no one and everyone. I had to get away from the news.

Early-morning fog had moved out, but the day was still cool and misty, and the moist air was soft on my face. The few houses strung along the bay side this far south were quiet early on a Sunday, the silence broken only by gently lapping waves and, now and then, the screech of a gull.

George was digging for octopus in the distance. I waved to him but didn't go any closer. I wasn't in the mood for sad-eyed octopuses.

I stepped through the weeds and sticker bushes that covered a point of land bounded by rubble and boulders jutting into the bay. Sometimes kids played baseball there with rude and noisy shouts of *"Batter! Batter!"* and *"Aww, yer blind!"* and *"My sisters' stockings run better than you!"* and the games would disintegrate into wrestling matches, but today the point was empty and peaceful. I scrambled down onto the rocks and sat, my feet in the water. Tiny waves splashed at my ankles. A pair of mallards glided past, the male's glossy green head glistening, and a cormorant dived for its breakfast, cleaving the water without a sound.

The water was cool and so clear I could see fish—minnows, smelt, tiny perch—darting by. Whiskered bullheads nibbled at my toes, so I took a slice of bread from my pocket, dropped crumbs into the water, and laughed as the fish sucked them in. I lay back against the rocks, feeling the morning sun on my face like a kiss, and drowsed.

Suddenly a squadron of navy planes soared above and dived. The roar of their engines ripped through the quiet morning and echoed in the silence. The very sound made the hair on my arms stand up.

I pulled my Book of Dead Things from my pocket. Along with my dead-fish drawings was a list of dead people, starting with my grandpa. I didn't really know him, but his name was Harry Morgan and he smelled sweet and smoky like his cigars. That much I remembered.

I needed to add the names of the poor navy fliers who'd died. *Brewer* was easy to spell, but I wasn't at all certain about *Jungjohann*. It seemed that the least I could do for the poor dead pilot was spell his name correctly.

I wrote the fliers' names right after President Roosevelt's mother; Florence's great-uncle Max, who, dizzy with excitement when the Dodgers won the pennant, fell off a streetcar; Lou Gehrig, the great first baseman, Pop's favorite player even if he was a Yankee; and Kazan the Wonder Dog from the movies. If the president's own mother and Lou Gehrig, "the Iron Horse," could die, why, then, anyone and anything could die. I still hadn't entered Gram's name onto the list of dead people. I didn't know why. I just couldn't. I shrugged and closed the book. I remembered her fine anyway.

On my way home I stopped at the Graysons' cottage. I'd heard a rumor that Mr. Grayson's nephew had been wounded in France. If he died, I could add him to the book. I needed to get more information from the Graysons without creeping them out. It was a delicate task.

They were sitting in beach chairs on their tiny front lawn, and Mrs. Grayson introduced me to her brother-in-law, Albert Wizzleskerkifizzlewitz or something really long and odd like that.

He popped up and gave me a tiny bow. "Pleased to meet you, ma'am," he said with a tip of his hat.

I tried not to snort. Albert was funny-looking. *Really* funny-looking. Bony and loose-limbed as if he were made of Popsicle sticks and paper clips. With his giant round head on a long skinny neck, he looked like a pumpkin on a pole. A pumpkin with a big nose. But his eyes were kind and his smile was wide.

"How's your nephew, Mr. Grayson?" I asked. "He isn't dead or anything, is he?"

Mr. and Mrs. Grayson exchanged glances before Mr. Grayson said, "No, he's okay. He'll have a limp for a while, but—"

"How about any of his soldier friends? Or anyone else?

I'm keeping an account of dead and lost people and things because . . . well, because my gram . . . because I'd forget . . . well, because." I looked down at my feet. It was hard to explain.

Mr. Grayson stared at me like I had three heads, but Albert said, "I get it. There's so much to worry about in this world and so little we can do about it. We have to watch over and remember what we can." And he smiled his warm smile.

I decided to like him.

Suddenly his eyes snapped and bulged out like Bugs Bunny's do when he sees something he wants, and he gulped a big gulp. I turned to see what had caused such a reaction.

Edna! It was Edna, tottering down Bayside Walk in a cloud of Jungle Gardenia with her arms full of grocery bags. Albert jumped up and stumbled to the walkway. "Let me help you with those bags, Mrs. . . ."

"It's *Miss*," said Edna, handing the bags to Albert. "*Miss* Duffy, and I think I'll rest here for a spell." She dropped into a chair next to Mrs. Grayson and smiled a cunning, teasing sort of smile at Albert. "You, sir, are a real gentleman." Albert's ears turned red, and he clutched at the grocery bags.

Was Edna flirting? How grotesque! Even though I hadn't collected anything dead for my book, I had to get away. "Nice to meet you, Mr. Wizzyfizz . . ."

"Just call me Albert," he said. Turning to Edna, he repeated in a sort of syrupy voice, "Just call me Albert."

Christopher Columbus!

"Sit yourself down," Mama said when I got back. "I have some news for you."

More news! More changes! More trouble! Holy mackerel! "What, is someone smellier than Edna moving in?" I flopped into a chair.

"That's unkind, Millie," Mama said. She pushed away the stack of coupons and box tops in front of her. Mama said she was a poet but mostly she wrote advertising jingles for prizes. "I heard from Rose McGrew that Vernon Fribble's brother's wife from Chicago is sick and has come to California for the healthy air." Mama lit a cigarette and dragged deeply. "She and her daughter are living with the Fribbles. You say you have no friends since Florence left. The girl's only a little older than you and won't know anyone here, so maybe you two could be friends."

I didn't need friends. I had Gram and Florence, even though they were gone, and didn't want any more. Besides, friends with a Fribble? Good gravy!

Mama actually thought she was helping me, trying to recruit friends for her hopeless daughter. Wasn't cutting out money-off coupons, writing jingles for free stuff, and spoiling Lily the pill keeping Mama busy enough? There already was hardly any time left for me and Pete. Pete didn't seem to mind—he had the Lone Ranger, after all—but I missed my mother. I missed spending time with her, just me and Mama, baking cookies and telling stories. Once when I was longing for a real Christmas like I'd read about in books, we sang carols, made snow angels in the sand, and had hot chocolate. But that was a long time ago. It seemed like Mama never saw me anymore unless she had bad news to share. And now she thought I could be friends with a Fribble.

"Sure, Mama, friends," I said, and rolled my eyes. "That's certainly a possibility." On my list right after marrying Icky Fribble and flying to the moon.

"Here," Mama said, "give me a hand with these." She shoved over scissors, a stack of magazines, and some empty box tops that she had collected from the few neighbors who didn't have to save ten cents on soap or get two boxes of CheeriOats for the price of one. My job was cutting the coupons from the magazines and matching them with the box tops. Hers was filling out entry forms and writing jingles to accompany them. I picked up the scissors and twirled them on my finger, then snipped haphazardly at my hair. "I wonder how I'd look in bangs."

"Quit fooling around and do something useful. And stop biting your fingernails." Mama sighed. "If Edna had a brain in her head, I could trust her to see to the house and you kids. I could get a job and not have to waste my life trying to find rhymes for *Budweiser* and *shredded wheat*." She chewed on her pencil. "Speaking of brains, mine seems to have dried up. What do you think of these jingles? Something poetic":

Six or eight or ten or teen,
At school and sports they're more than keen.
Healthier kids you've never seen
Because they drink their Ovaltine.

I frowned. Corny.

"Or something simple: *Maxwell House coffee, too good to be just for breakfast*."

"Boring, Mama. And ordinary. What about . . ." I waved the scissors in the air and sang, *"Eat Sunsweet prunes both morns and noons to keep your bowel from crying foul!"*

"Don't be vulgar, Millie." There was more pencil chewing and paper shuffling from Mama. "Look at this one, a contest with a prize of cash money—two dollars! They want one hundred words or less on why your house needs air freshener."

"I can do it in two words," I said, scissoring loudly. "Cousin Edna."

OCTOBER 12, 1941
SUNDAY

The day was warm, the sun bright, and the tide high. In the old days, Pop would grill hot dogs on a day like this, and Mama would make macaroni salad and Kool-Aid freezer pops. I'd talk Pop into swimming with me and we'd race to the Lempkes' dock and back. He usually let me win. Now hot dogs are a frill, Pop is too tired and worried to swim, and fun is hard to come by.

I scoured the beach for things for my book, but pickings were slim—a couple of mussel shells and a sand crab. Icky Fribble's older brother, the dumb Dwayne, and his even dumber friends were acting stupid, shoving and splashing each other in the water. A flock of girls giggled and squealed and flipped their hair as they watched. When did girls get so dumb? Hit junior high, and your brains turn to mush at the sight of skinny boys in bathing suits. Good gravy!

I pulled our rowboat into the water and climbed aboard with a jelly sandwich and *Little Women* from the library. Facing the stern of the boat, I dipped the oars and rowed. The rhythmic motions were slow and calming, soothingly repetitious, and the boat glided on the water like a great sea-bird. All was quiet out there, with only the sound of splashing against the bow and the oars clacking in the oarlocks as they slipped in and out of the water. A seagull circled silently overhead but paid me no mind, as if I were part of the bay, and the sky, and the creatures in it.

The sun on my back relaxed my shoulders and my thoughts. I belonged to the bay, and it to me, and for a moment all was well.

When I reached a spot where the bay was calm and smooth, I rested the oars. The water was so clear here you could see all the way to the bottom. Hundreds of sand dollars, wedged on edge into the sandy floor, swayed in unison as the water moved over them, and a bright orange garibaldi drifted by. There was no war talk out here. No Mama trying to find enough coupons for dinner. No Pop failing to find a real job. No Lily having a bad day. No Cousin Edna.

The boat bobbed on the water as I finished my sandwich. The sun warmed me into sleepiness and I lay back, eyes closed. There was boysenberry jelly on my hands and my face and my book—Gram's jelly, made from her own berries. It tasted like summer. There would be no more jelly now that Gram was gone.

Once Gram and I made gingerbread for Christmas. She said it was a good thing for girls to know, like songs of protest and the phone number of your state representative. She tied a towel over my dress for an apron and put me in charge of sifting flour. It drifted around me, and I imagined a gentle snowstorm falling.

Lily had wanted to come to Gram's, too, but I annoyed

her into a wheezing fit so I was able to go by myself. Gram rode out to the beach and shepherded me back to her apartment. When we left, Lily was cuddled in Mama's lap and Mama was crooning some sweet song to her. A twinge of jealousy pinched me, but I would have Gram all to myself.

Gram pulled out the cinnamon and cloves and allspice and added them to the flour and sugar with the eggs and buttermilk. "A little spice, a little sweet, and a tiny bit of sour. Just like life," she said.

Lily was the sour in my life, I thought as I whisked the batter. "Gram," I asked, "how come Mama loves Lily best?"

"Millie, you had your mama all to yourself for five years before Lily came along. Don't begrudge Lily her share now. There's plenty of love in your house for all of you."

"Still . . ." I started to argue but decided I didn't want to waste precious time with Gram talking about Lily.

We ate the gingerbread warm with cold glasses of milk. To my taste, the gingerbread could have been a little sweeter, but that was true of my life, too, I thought as I chewed.

When I finished, Gram patted my cheek and smiled. I could almost feel her soft hand on my face now.

I sat up, startled. There was something in the water, stroking through the bay. It wasn't a seal. Not big enough to be one of the surfers. Who or what could it be?

A splash sounded and a face popped up. The face wore goggles filled with water, but I recognized the yellow hair and red, peeling nose. No, not a seal but Dicky Fribble.

"Well, cut off my legs and call me Shorty, if it ain't Mil-dreadful, the pride of the McGargles."

"Hello, Icky. Let go of my boat and go drown yourself."
I turned to my book.

"My brother, Dwayne, says the Nazis have invented an invincible secret weapon and they'll be here before Christmas. That scare you, Mil-barge?" he asked with a splash.

"Knock it off. You're ruining a library book. And Nazis don't scare me half as much as your face."

"Better get yourself some leather pants and learn to yodel. The Nazis are coming. *Jawohl, jawohl, heil Hitler!*" *Splash.* "Be seein' ya." With another splash he was gone.

"Not if I see you first," I muttered.

Were the Nazis really coming here? Our house would be an easy target—just aim for the Sweeneys' big pine. I rowed in and beached the boat. As I ran for home, hungry gulls soared and dived above me like bomber planes.

Pete was sitting in front of our house surrounded by hills of snow. No, not snow. Toilet paper. He was unrolling it as fast as fog moving in on a gloomy June morning.

"What are you doing?" I asked, gathering up armfuls of paper.

He held out two empty cardboard tubes. "I'm making binoculars. Me and Ralphie and MeToo are watching for German ships coming into the bay."

Gee whiz. Even five-and-a-half-year-olds were obsessed with the possibility of war. "Better to watch for Mama. She'll have kittens if she sees you ruining all this toilet paper." I tried to roll the paper onto the tubes again but finally gave them back to Pete and stuffed the paper into the trash can. "Besides, ships can't sail into the bay. It's too shallow, especially at low tide."

"Help me, Millie."

"I just did."

"No, help me stick these tubes together so they're real binoculars."

I got masking tape from the kitchen and taped the tubes together. "If I were you, I wouldn't let Mama see them. She'll charge you five cents a roll for the wasted paper."

Pete held the cardboard binoculars to his eyes. "Don't worry. I'll be able to see her coming from a mile away." He trotted off to find Ralphie and MeToo, who were making their own binoculars. There probably wasn't a roll of toilet paper left in Mission Beach.

In the kitchen the radio was broadcasting the war news that was becoming the background music of my life. Mama saw my face and said, "Enough," and turned it off.

"Mama, do you think the war will really come here? Why can't Hitler be satisfied with all of Europe?"

"Come on, Millie, we can't let him have Europe. He's doing awful things. Sooner or later America will have to fight him."

"I sure hope it's later. Much later. Like when I'm already dead."

"I'll telegraph the president and ask him to hold off on declaring war for a hundred years. That do?"

I nodded.

Mama rummaged in the icebox. "Want one?" she asked, and she handed me a carrot.

Pete came skidding in. "I'm hungry. Not carrot hungry. *Really* hungry."

Mama ruffled his hair. "How about I make you half a peanut butter sandwich?"

"Skippy with lettuce and mayonnaise."

"Weird but okay."

Pete took a couple of bites. "That's enough." He burped, and his face was pale and pinched. "I feel seasick."

"You don't look too well," said Mama. She felt his forehead and his cheeks.

"Maybe it's the worms," Pete said.

"What worms?"

"Millie said you'd charge me five cents a roll for the two rolls of toilet paper I used, and I didn't have two nickels." Mama frowned at me. I shrugged. "Billy Martin said he'd give me a nickel for each worm I ate. I ate three." He handed Mama three nickels. "You can have the extra nickel, too." Then he took a deep breath and vomited peanut butter, lettuce, and bits of worm over my bare feet! Christopher Columbus!

Mama took Pete on her lap. "No more worm eating. You've paid enough for your foolishness." She looked at my bespattered feet. "Both of you."

OCTOBER 18, 1941
SATURDAY

Rattling windows woke me way too early. It was a Santa Ana, the hot, dry wind that heats the land and stirs up the ocean, leaving folks edgy and jumpy. My skin was itchy and my head ached. I lay in bed grumbling until—holy cow! With the wind whipping up the waves, the surfers would be out! Especially one particular surfer, Rocky Boynton.

I pulled on my bathing suit, grabbed a bucket in case I found dead things for my book, and raced out the door before anyone could wake up and want me. The wind tossed my hair and the blowing sand stung my face. The washing that the Dexters across the alley had on the line danced crazily in the wind. A green shirt blew off and did cartwheels across their yard.

My eyes filled with sand. I tiptoed back into the house and found some swimming goggles. Fastening them around my head, I hurried back outside. That was better. I tore through the alleys and across Mission Boulevard to the ocean-side beach near Queenstown Court, where the lifeguards and surfers hung out.

And there they were. Or more important, there *he* was. The tall fellow with wavy hair and a smile like a toothpaste ad. The one called Rocky. It was hard to believe he and Pete and Icky were the same species. Rocky was no skinny, pimply-faced kid. He was a dreamboat. I could feel my pulse pounding in my throat as I watched him.

He carried his heavy wooden board under one arm as easily as if it were a loaf of bread. Such muscles. I shook my head. "Get hold of yourself, Millie," I muttered.

Rocky strode to the water and plunged in, working his way through the waves. Far from shore, just before the waves were breaking, he climbed onto the board, belly down. When a large wave rolled up behind him, he paddled hard, caught the wave, and pushed himself up as the face of the wave lifted his board and carried it at top speed toward the shore. Flying on the crest of the wave, he looked like some Greek god walking on the water. Over and over he paddled out and rode in again, the sun glinting on his wet skin. Between the hot wind and Rocky's magnificence, the air felt electric. I swore I could feel my hair frizz.

There were other surfers in the water, but once Rocky left, I stopped watching. What was the point? Instead I walked the beach, gathering dead things in my bucket for my book: sand crabs, sea snails, and what looked like the skull of a bird or a snake or a very small dragon.

"Out of the way, McGargle." It was Icky, and he kicked sand at me as he passed.

"Nincompoop!" I shouted after him.

Icky dropped his shirt, shoes, socks, and towel on the sand and headed into the water, to annoy the surfers, no doubt.

I grinned. I had a sudden, super idea. A genius idea. An Einstein of an idea.

Taking handfuls of crabs and snails from my pail—the dragon skull I kept to draw later—I shoved them into the toes of Icky's socks and packed them tight. Slimy, stinky shells crackled and oozed, and the smell was awful. I put the socks back with Icky's other things, moved some ways away, lay down on the sand, and waited.

I'd almost given up when Icky finally came out of the water. *Put your socks on right here,* I messaged him from my mind, but he just slipped his shoes onto his bare feet, wrapped his shirt and socks in his towel, and turned for home.

What a fizzle. No fun at all. It was getting way too hot anyway. Going to be a scorcher. I picked up my empty pail, wrote **McGONIGLE** in the sand twice for luck, and then headed back home against the sharp and sandy wind that burned my cheeks and clattered on my goggles.

Back on Bayside Walk I saw a girl standing in front of the Fribbles' house. She was a bit older than me, red-haired and pale, and a stranger. Suddenly she shouted, in a voice like a bullhorn, "I hate Dicky Fribble!"

"Who doesn't?" I told her. "But call him Icky. That really irritates him."

She grinned and bellowed, "I hate Icky Fribble and Dicky Fribble, too!"

"What did he do to you?"

"He locked me out of the house."

"You live here? With the Fribbles? Who are—"

"Rosemary Fribble, get yourself in here!" shouted Mrs.

Fribble in her thin, shrill voice. "Stop shouting like a loon. What will the neighbors think?"

"I guess she made Dicky open the door," said the girl, who was apparently Rosemary Fribble. "See you." And she ran for the house.

I was speechless. Rosemary Fribble. This was Mrs. Fribble's niece? Was Rosemary as bad as the rest of the Fribbles, or was she trapped like a princess in a house full of ogres? I wondered if I could find out without having to talk to a Fribble.

The others were finishing breakfast when I got home.

"I just saw the Fribble girl," I said, picking at the toast crusts on the table.

"That's nice," said Mama. She slurped her coffee and added, "You've missed breakfast. We've eaten everything."

"Here, Millie, have some of my special raisin toast." Pete handed me a cold slice spread with something thick and red.

"What's this on it?"

"Jelly," said Pete.

"Looks funny," I said, and took a bite. "It's ketchup! Christopher Columbus, that's awful!"

"Ketchup is tomato jelly," Pete said. "I like it." And he scowled.

"No squabbles." Pop stood up from the table and stretched. "Who wants to go fish from the bridge?"

"I do! I do!" said Lily and Pete together.

I shook my head. "Not me. As soon as I brush the tomato jelly out of my mouth, I have homework."

I retreated to the bedroom, where Edna was tying a scarf

into a turban around her hair and whistling. "I have a date," she said.

I flopped onto the bed. "Is it Moe, Larry, or Curly?" I apparently was speaking to her again.

She snickered. "That would be fun, but it's none of the Stooges. I'm seeing Albert, and he's not a bit of fun. Pretty funny-looking, too, but he does buy a good lunch, and he's nuts about me." She winked and turned for the bathroom.

She was back not a minute later, pot of rouge in her hand. "I forgot where I'm going."

"You're seeing Albert."

"Why?" Edna asked.

"He's buying you lunch."

Edna snapped her fingers. "That's right!" And with a grin, she returned to the bathroom.

Ever since Harold had been a no-show and a disappointment, Mama worried about the type of guys Edna was encouraging. Now Mama insisted that Edna's dates pick her up at home so Mama could look them over and make sure Edna would be all right. Even if they were relatives of neighbors like Albert was. Mama treated Edna almost like a daughter, an older daughter, and I felt a familiar stab of jealousy.

When Albert knocked, I let him in. "Albert," Mama said as she entered. "I'm Lois McGonigle, Edna's cousin." She didn't seem at all surprised or amused at Albert's appearance, which was just as odd as I remembered.

"Pleased, ma'am," Albert said with a nod. His voice was deep and soft and filled the room.

"Leave us, Millie, please," Mama said. "Albert and I have to talk."

"But, Mama . . ."

"Go, Millie."

I stomped into the bedroom. Gee whiz! I never got to be in on interesting talk.

"And close the door," Mama called after me.

Even with the door closed, I could hear murmuring and a word here and there: *no sense, forgetful, vulnerable* from Mama. And in Albert's soft rumble: *simple, fresh, shelter,* and *protect*.

Albert must have passed Mama's test because I heard her knock on the bathroom door and say, "Enough primping, Edna. Albert is waiting."

With muted laughter and more murmured words, Edna was off on her date.

I curled up on the bed to start my homework. For history, the sixth grade at Mission Bay Elementary was studying Europe in the Middle Ages. Hitler was breathing down our necks, and I had to spend time in the eleventh century, when England was being invaded by marauding Vikings. Skippy Morrison, who was obsessed with fire, said Vikings burned whole towns and all their inhabitants, put their own dead in boats set afire, and sent them out to sea.

Murder and fighting, towns destroyed, people dead. Just like now but without the bombs. Christopher Columbus! Was history nothing but war and death? My only escape was a nap.

When I woke, it was nearly dinnertime. Mama was washing lettuce, and the radio was broadcasting the latest war news. The destroyer USS *Kearny* had been torpedoed by German U-boats near Iceland. Although Iceland was far, far away from San Diego, the war seemed closer every day. My face grew cold, and I began to gnaw on my thumbnail.

Mama frowned, but said only, "Stop biting your nails, and I'll change the station. No more war talk." She twisted the dial and from the radio came the story of the Barbours of San Francisco—*One Man's Family.*

Yes. A soap opera. Just the thing. These pretend troubles were much easier than real troubles. At the commercial, I asked Mama, "What's for dinner?"

"Your pop had good luck fishing today."

I poured myself a glass of milk and flopped into a chair. "Fish again? I'm going to develop gills. Shouldn't dinner mean roast beef or chicken sometimes?"

"Well, when you earn enough money to keep this family in roast beef and chicken, we'll eat it. Until then we're grateful for what the bay provides and your pop catches."

"What is it tonight? Bass? Corvina? Anything but perch, I hope."

"Perch," said my mother.

Of course. I banged my head onto the table.

"If you want other fish, go and catch some. You can do more than just sit and whine," Mama said. "There's small halibut out there, flounder and bass, mullet and sculpin. Clams and scallops and oysters. The bay offers us plenty to eat besides perch, if you'd just make the effort. Do something to contribute. You catch our dinner for tomorrow."

"It'll still be fish."

Mama huffed. "Just do it. I mean it." She put the lettuce in a salad bowl with celery and tomato chunks. "Here's something you'll enjoy. I just saw Bertha Fribble at Bell's

Grocery. She said Dicky came home from the beach this morning stinking worse than the bay at low tide, so she threw his clothes into the washer with the other laundry. When she ran them through the wringer, pieces of smashed crab and various vile things were stuck everywhere, in the towels and sheets and Mr. Fribble's work shirts."

My belly filled with silent laughter.

"Dicky said he had no idea how that happened, but he had to scour the washer and the wringer and then wash all the clothes again. And they still smelled." Making her voice loud and squeaky just like Mrs. Fribble's, Mama added, "Poor Richard is in a heap of trouble."

Icky in trouble? This was too much for me. I snorted, and milk spewed out of my nose. Then *I* was in trouble. But it was worth it.

OCTOBER 19, 1941
SUNDAY

It was early but the sun was up and so was I. I was on a mission. "Good morning, Cap, I'm Millie McGonigle," I said when he opened the door to the fishing shack out near the jetty that was his home.

Captain Charlie looked like Roy Rogers's sidekick, Gabby Hayes, bewhiskered and scrawny, except Gabby Hayes needed a haircut and Captain Charlie was bald as a baby bird. What I could see of his face under his whiskers was as wrinkled as his clothes, and his clothes were plenty wrinkled. I'd heard he'd been living here since he got out of the army after the Civil War, which would make him very old and the shack even older.

"I know you," he said, leaning against the porch rail. "You're Martin McGonigle's kid. Seen you around but never formally made your acquaintance. How d'ya do." He stuck out a rough, gnarled hand and we shook.

"I hoped you might help me with something, Cap. My mama wants me to fish for our dinner but I'm sick of fish. Baked fish. Fried fish. Fish cakes. Fish stew."

"Seems to me, you have to catch what's in the water, lass," and his mustache twitched. "Never heard of a soul baiting a hook and catching a T-bone steak in Mission Bay."

"Sure wish you could, but no, I want to catch abalone like you used to." I'd show Mama I didn't just sit and whine. She'd have to admit that. But I wasn't going to catch just any old fish. "I remember Pop coming home with abalone once in a while, saying you'd caught too many and were sharing them with us. They were yummy and not fishlike at all."

"Ahh, them days are as gone as my hair." He rubbed his head. "So what can I do you for?"

"Tell me where and how to catch them."

"Well, young Millie, you're a tall drink of water but a deal too slight to be fighting ocean swells and diving down to cut abalone off rocks."

"I could try, and I'd be very careful. Where would I start?"

He pulled on his whiskers and *hmmm*ed a moment. "La Jolla Cove was always lucky for me. The big rocks out beyond the breakers should have plenty of abalone clinging to them. If the tide is low enough, you might be able to reach some without having to dive down into the deeper water. Then you'd have to cut them off the rocks with a fish knife and pry them from their shells."

"Would a steak knife do? We certainly don't need it for steak."

"Mebbe, but I don't like it. Don't seem a suitable pursuit for a girl."

I shrugged. This girl was going to try anyway.

"What'd your folks say?"

I shrugged again. I didn't know what Mama or Pop would say, so I didn't ask them.

Pop was gone when I got back and Mama was hanging laundry outside. Lily and Pete were arguing over a coloring book. Pete refused to color inside the lines. "It cramps my style," he said. Who knew where he got these things?

I put a coat on over my bathing suit and grabbed Pop's fishing waders, goggles, a steak knife, and a sack to carry my catch home. My mouth actually watered as I thought of us pounding the abalone meat thin, coating it with egg and flour, and frying it up. And the big shell lined with colorful mother-of-pearl was just right for keeping sea glass or hairpins or pennies in, if you had pennies. Which I didn't.

I did have two dimes, change from getting groceries last week, which was just enough to get me to La Jolla and back. I caught the bus at the amusement center and climbed aboard, juggling the wading boots, goggles, knife, and burlap sack. A piercing squeak called, "Millieeee!" and a hand grabbed the sleeve of my coat. Good gravy. Mrs. Fribble, mother to Icky and the dreadful Dwayne!

"Millie!" she squeaked again. "Sit here. I'll shove over."

So I did, crowding in with my equipment, resigned to sharing the bus ride with Mrs. Fribble.

"Where on earth are you off to this morning?" she squealed, and people turned around to look. "I myself am going to Dunaway's Pharmacy in Pacific Beach for Mr. Fribble's sister's medicine. Lillian has used hers up and the Mission Beach Pharmacy is out, so I have to take myself up to Pacific Beach. Lillian is ailing, poor thing—weak lungs, terrible, terrible, like your sister, terrible. She and my niece Rosemary will be with us awhile. The house is so crowded, but she's family, so what can I do? Makes too much work for me and my poor suffering feet."

She paused to take a breath and I jumped in. "I think I saw your niece once. Tall with red hair?"

"Yes, that's her. Big-city girl with big-city ways. She doesn't get along with my Richard and Dwayne. Too citified and surly. One house, one family, I say. No freeloading relatives. Like that cousin of yours. Edna. Spouting German and acting suspicious. I wouldn't be at all surprised if she wasn't some sort of spy or . . ."

Blah blah blah, she went, while I stared out the window, trying to decide whether to jump through it.

"Pull the cord for me, Millie," she said at last. "This is my stop. I have to get off and take my poor suffering feet to the pharmacy, as if I had nothing else to do." I pulled the cord happily. Mrs. Fribble climbed over me and got off the bus, still muttering, and lumbered away on her poor suffering feet. I sat back and rested my poor suffering ears! And what did she mean about Cousin Edna being a spy? If Edna had secret spy information, she'd forget it in a second. Some spy.

As we left Pacific Beach, the small houses and empty lots gradually became green parklike sites with large deep-roofed bungalows covered with flowers like cottages in a fairy tale. High jagged cliffs behind and between them rose from the sea. *Toto, I've a feeling we're not in Mission Beach anymore,* I said to myself.

The farther we drove into La Jolla, the bigger the houses

and more numerous the hotels and fancy shops and big buildings in the same sort of Spanish style as the museums in Balboa Park. I got off on Prospect and walked along the winding road and over the massive rocks between the town and the sea.

Cliffs made of huge boulders flung into the water as if by giants nearly surrounded the beach. I could see sea lions lounging on the rocks and barking. And I sure could smell them. It stunk almost like the mudflats at home.

It was a crisp, cloudy day with a wind that blew cool and damp from the sea. Here and there, people sat on the small patch of sand with their faces to the sky, searching for a bit of warm sunshine, and a fisherman in a green hat was casting lines, but there was no one with goggles and a knife except me.

The tide was out, but swells that rolled in all the way from Hawaii or Japan or some other South Seas island still crashed and sprayed on the shore. The waves were big and powerful, their sound was booming, and I was scared but determined to show Mama I could do something useful. I took off my coat, put on Pop's waders and the goggles, and slogged out through the waves. The beach dropped steeply and the water got deep fast. Breaking waves splashed over me, soaking me and filling the boots with icy seawater. *Slosh, slosh,* I went, until the next big wave pushed me back to where I'd started.

I brushed my wet hair off my face, drained the goggles, and sloshed out again. It took me many minutes to trudge a very few feet through the cold and churning water. When I finally shoved past the breaking waves, I fought my way closer to the boulders that lined the cove. Sticking my head and hands in the water and trying to keep my balance, I felt for abalone clinging to the rocks but found only rock.

Farther and farther out I waded, and the water grew deeper and the waves stronger. A giant wave knocked me down, tore the sack from my hand, and washed it away. My mouth and nose filled with salt water, and I gagged, spit, and spluttered as I fought the powerful undertow that tried to drag me out to sea. I kicked and paddled furiously, and the next wave washed me back to shore.

I pulled off the waders filled with water and dumped them on the beach. They must have weighed a zillion pounds and certainly weren't keeping my feet dry. As I started to *slosh, slosh* back beyond the breakers once again, my arm was grabbed from behind. "No, you ain't," said a gruff voice. It was the green-hatted fisherman from down the beach. "You want to get washed all the way to China? This water's too rough for you."

I shrugged off his hand but I didn't go back in the water. "I guess you're right," I said. This wasn't my best idea ever. The waves were too strong, the biggest boulders too far out, and the water too cold. And the abalone apparently clung to rocks much deeper than I could reach. I'd have to be able to breathe underwater. Captain Charlie didn't tell me that.

I took off the goggles, picked up the boots, put my coat on over my cold, soggy bathing suit, stuck the unused knife in my pocket, and, disheartened, headed for home.

Climbing up to the road was harder than climbing down. As I trudged back to the bus stop, the fisherman, toting three small burlap sacks and a fishing pole, was right ahead of me. I stared at his loot and sighed. I was cold and dripping wet, bedraggled and empty-handed. I sighed again.

He stopped and said, "Say, missy, you sound like you lost your best friend."

"Worse," I told him. "I went out to catch us supper and I failed and have to tell my mama that I have nothing."

"You're Martin McGonigle's girl, ain't you? Your pop and I used to fish together. You tell him Smitty says hey."

When we reached Prospect Street, I could see the bus coming. I nodded to the fisherman and prepared to board. "Hold on there now, missy," he said. "I had fine luck today— the fish were just begging to take my hook. Two sacks are enough for me. You'd be doing me a favor if you take one."

He handed me a sack. Likely not abalone, but it was still supper. "Gee, thanks, Mr. Smitty," I said, and climbed aboard the bus and sat.

Not wanting to seem greedy, I didn't look in the sack until the bus had pulled away from Smitty.

Perch.

It was *perch*. Three of them. Seemed perch lived in the ocean as well as the bay. Christopher Columbus, I was cursed!

I sat there, cold and clammy and smelling of fish. The odor got stronger as the bus got warmer and more crowded. People began frowning and looking around for the source of the stink, so I frowned and looked around, too, as if saying, *Who could that inconsiderate person with the fish smell be?*

I shivered as I walked home. Mission Bay might be paradise, but it was no place for a girl in a wet bathing suit on a breezy October day. Once home, I stripped down, washed off the sand and salt in the tub, and pulled on pants and a sweater.

Pop was on Lily's bed reading to her. "Where's Mama?" I asked. I was eager to show her the dinner I'd caught, even though I didn't really catch it and it was just perch.

"You remember Mama's old friend from North Park, Billie Harlow," he said. "Her son Garland is having a birthday party, so Mama took Pete over. Pete drew a picture of the Lone Ranger for a present, and your mama taped a nickel to it."

"You know," I said, "Pete will have that nickel off and into his pocket before they get anywhere near Garland."

Pop shook his head but smiled. "That's my boy."

My fishing expedition had left me exhausted. Almost drowning was enough to tire anyone, but I still had to turn Smitty's perch into dinner. I was cleaning the fish in the kitchen when Pop came in. I told him how I got the fish and gave him the *hey* from Smitty.

"Good old Smitty. Where'd you run into him?"

I shrugged. "At the beach." Pop didn't ask where exactly, and I sure didn't bring it up.

He took the remains of the fish to the garbage can and washed his hands. "I had some extra shifts at the Burger Shack this week, and I think we deserve a treat. How about you and Lily and I go see the new Cary Grant movie?"

I was never too tired for a movie. I stashed the cleaned perch in the icebox. Then, hands washed and hair and teeth brushed in record time, I hurried to the door. "Come on, let's go," I called.

But no one came—only the sound of wheezing and

coughing, Pop murmuring, and Lily mumbling tearfully. I knew what that meant. No movie today. I made a face in Lily's direction.

"Too much excitement," said Pop when he came out. He put his arm around my shoulders. He smelled like pipe smoke and burgers.

"Millie, tell me a story," Lily called from the other room.

"Not now," I shouted back. "I'm not in the mood." I dropped onto the sofa and Pop sat next to me. "It burns me up, Pop," I muttered through clenched teeth. "Weren't we doing just fine without her seven years ago, just you and me and Mama? Why did you have to go and mess it up by having Lily?"

"Millie, you don't mean that."

"I do. Christopher Columbus! I'm tired of missing out on things because of Lily. Remember last year when we were going to the zoo? Lily threw up and we stayed home. In June we went to Balboa Park for a picnic for Gram's birthday. Remember? Lily had an attack right there at the park. She wheezed and coughed all the way home on the trolley. People moved away from us like we had the plague or something. Pop, it was utterly humiliating."

Pop got his pipe from his shirt pocket. "I know it's hard on you. I could give you the money for the bus and a movie ticket, but I don't like the idea of you going by yourself. With hundreds of the new workers at the airplane plant and all the naval activity, there are so many strangers in town. I wouldn't feel right."

I didn't tell him I'd already been to La Jolla and back that day with lots of strangers. Pop thinks I'm still a kid. If he asked, I'd have to tell him, but I was volunteering nothing.

He stuck his pipe between his teeth and lit it. "I'm sorry. I know you'd enjoy the movie, and we don't often have enough money for . . . I don't make enough . . . Jobs are . . ." He fell silent and puffed on his pipe.

I had a new worry. What if no one bought burgers anymore and the Burger Shack didn't need Pop? What if we ran out of money? What if we were poor from now on? What if I had to go to school in rags?

Pop looked old for a minute, with his sagging cheeks and sad eyes. No joking around today. Taking a deep breath, I decided to let up on him a little. "It's not your fault we don't have money, Pop. You didn't cause the Depression or lose the store on purpose." I took his hand. "Still, people, even poor people, sometimes need what Mama calls frills to keep our chins up. And then when we plan for them, Lily keeps us home."

Talking to Pop like that was weird, but I appreciated him listening and not telling me to cheer up. I huddled close, breathing deeply of his sweet-smelling tobacco. I supposed you could call tobacco a frill but I said nothing. Pop felt bad enough.

Instead I pinched my lips and went outside to throw stones. Into the bay. And the sky. And at the window in the bedroom. "Take that, Lily, you killjoy," I muttered. "I hope your doll's stuffing all leaks out!"

I felt better.

OCTOBER 26, 1941
SUNDAY

T he morning was cloudy with a promise of sunshine. I pulled a sweater on over my bathing suit, put my book in the pocket, and headed out. Pickings on the beach were slim, but I found a few sand crabs and part of a jellyfish. It was hard to believe it was a living thing. Or had been. It looked more like pale jelly or a slimy cloud. Odd and interesting. I drew it carefully in my book. Finally I signed **McGONIGLE** in the mud and turned for home.

"Hi," called someone running up beside me. "I'm Rosemary Fribble, but I guess you know that already. Call me Rosie. Aunt Bertha told me to get lost, so I packed some sandwiches and grapes for a picnic. Want to join me?"

I hesitated. She was a Fribble, after all.

"They're peanut butter and bacon," she said.

Bacon? I hardly remembered the taste of bacon. It was a frill. This Fribble hated Icky and had bacon. She could very well become a friend. "Sure," I said. "Do you want to run home and change first?"

"Why? What's wrong?"

"Those," I said, gesturing to her wool plaid skirt and saddle shoes. "They're not exactly beach-picnic wear."

"My legs are cold, and I don't like walking barefoot on stones and sticker plants. It hurts my feet. I'm fine the way I am."

I shook my head. Hurt feet? My own bare feet were summer-tough all year round. I could walk on stones and stickers and maybe even glass. We beach kids are proud of that. "Okay," I said. "Let me grab something for us to drink and I'll be right back."

And I was, with a thermos of lemonade and towels to sit on. "Let's go to the island. It's right out in the bay. I'll row."

"Wow. You have a boat?" Rosie asked. And then, "Aw, birds!" she said as a flock of gulls flew past. "Hey, birdies, are you hungry?" She tossed a handful of grapes into the air.

"No, don't!" I shouted, but it was too late. A swarm of gulls, screeching and fighting, raced in, circling us and diving for food. One swept close to Rosie's hair, and she flapped her arms and screeched even louder than the birds.

I thought the scene pretty funny, but it was obvious that Rosie wasn't enjoying it. "Scat! Scat!" I hollered, chasing them and waving a towel. "Get away, you flying rats!" That's what Mama always says.

The tide was turning, and the weather was clearing. We climbed into the boat and I rowed in silence until we reached a spot where the bay was smooth and deep. I rested the oars, and a calm feeling settled over me like a soft cloud as we bobbed.

"I'm sorry your mama is sick," I told Rosie.

"Thanks. She's doing a little better. The fresh sea air helps her."

"How do you like living with the Fribbles?"

"Are you kidding? Uncle Vernon's okay but he's never home, and can you blame him? The others are horrid." A flock of gulls squawked by. Rosie watched them for a minute and said, "Sorry for being a baby back there. The birds scared me. We don't have seagulls in my part of Chicago."

"What *do* you have?"

"Pigeons. Lots of pigeons. And robins. Sometimes you can see a hawk. And Bears and Cubs."

"You mean in a zoo?"

"That was a joke. They're sports teams. And we have skyscrapers forty stories and more, trains that run on rails in the sky, mansions on Lake Shore Drive, fancy stores on Michigan Avenue where you can buy anything you want." She took a deep breath before continuing. "There's a planetarium, where you can lie back and watch the movements of the stars and planets on the ceiling, and the Field Museum, with Egyptian mummies and—"

"Enough, enough. I'm just a country bumpkin," I said, "overwhelmed by the wonders of the big city. But I can tell you miss it." I dunked my feet into the water and kicked softly. "Mission Beach might not have mummies and skyscrapers and fancy stores, but I love the feel of the morning sun on my face, the misty air on a cloudy day, the sound of the foghorn." I looked around at the bay and the beach and smiled. "I like the warm sand on sunny days and the way early-morning fog surrounds me, shelters me, like I was in a snow globe."

"Gee, Millie," Rosie said with a sigh. "That's almost poetry. You're a real Laura Ingalls Wilder."

Not such a country bumpkin after all, I thought. I rowed the rest of the way to the island, where I beached the boat and we climbed out. The island was sandy, its dunes speckled with scrubby grasses, pickleweed and bearberry, and sticker bushes. I took Rosie to my favorite spot, the small pond where you could sit on driftwood and dunk your feet in the water. I called it a lagoon, like Jon Hall found in *South of Pago Pago,* so I hummed "Lovely Hula Hands" while we settled.

A salty breeze blew in from the west. The island was quiet and peaceful and empty. Sitting in a sunny spot with our backs against a beached log, Rosie and I ate her sandwiches. "I needed this," I said. "My sister, Lily, is feeling really bad today. When she struggles to breathe, it's like she's sucking all the air out of the house." I wrinkled up my nose. "The whole place stinks of Vicks VapoRub, Jungle Gardenia, and Edna's fried Spam. I had to get out."

"Same with my mother, but it must be harder on a little kid." Rosie licked peanut butter off her fingers. "I'd love to have a little sister. The only relatives I have are my brother, Leo the goon, and Dwayne and Dicky Fribble. Talk about stinking up the house. Do you have fun with Lily? Play games and tell her stories?"

"Nah. I avoid her as much as I can. Lily's a pill. Besides, she's sick all the time. That's why we moved to the beach. I love the beach but I'd trade Lily for a dog any day."

"But you're her big sister."

"Phooey. She's still a pill. Like this: the Randalls' dog had puppies. Six soft and cuddly puppies!" I flung my hands up.

"I really wanted one. I'd call her Sophronia, after the girl in *The Five Little Peppers*, but no. No dogs. Lily's allergic. Instead I got a goldfish. Pete flushed it down the toilet. He was teaching it to swim."

Rosie laughed, leaned back, and lifted her face to the sun. "I think you should give her a break. Lily may be a pill but she can't be as bad as my cousin, the beastly Dicky. He could have been the model for the obnoxious Tootsie McSnoots in the *Little Orphan Annie* comic strip."

I snorted. "I remember her. We should call Dicky *Icky McSnoots*. Or maybe *Icky Snooks,* after bratty Baby Snooks. I used to listen to her on *Maxwell House Coffee Time* at my friend Florence's house before she moved away. So funny." I giggled, remembering. "Baby Snooks is why Florence and I invented the wet-diaper scale. Once Florence peed in her pants from laughing at her. Ever after, something really funny we'd call a wet-diaper event. The range is one to three."

"I'll bet I got two diapers when I went loco over the seagulls," Rosie said.

"On the button," I said, tapping my nose.

Rosie smiled. "What's on the other side of the island?"

"Follow me!" We raced up a small rise, tripping over rocks and stones and clumps of dry grass.

Rosie got there first. "I see water. And sandbars. And a motorboat on the beach," she said. "And . . . Millie, there's someone there. A man. He's doing exercises—touching his toes and, oh, Millie, he doesn't have any clothes on! Quick! Come look."

I peeked around her shoulder and, with a squeal, dropped

to the ground. "It's Rocky! And I think he saw us. Get down! Get down!"

Rosie laughed, but I slithered away on my belly, *ooh*ing and *oof*ing over stickers and rocks. "Whoever Rocky is, he won't recognize us," Rosie called to me. "We're strangers."

"I'm not. He knows me. At least he's seen me. I think."

We finally scrambled back to the beach. "We need to get out of here fast." I jumped into the boat, and Rosie followed. I rowed furiously, yanking so hard at the oars that one of the oarlocks snapped right off.

"Holy moly! Now what?" I tried rowing with one oar, but that only took us in circles.

The wind was rising and the day grew cooler. And the boat began drifting, not toward the beach but toward the channel and the Ocean Beach bridge and then the open sea.

"I can swim back to shore and get help," Rosie said. "I had swimming lessons at summer camp last year."

"I'll have drifted to China before you get there and back."

"We could both swim back to shore."

"I don't want to abandon the boat."

"We could tow the boat."

"No, we couldn't."

"You're right. We couldn't, but those are all the ideas I have. What'll we do?"

As we got closer to the bridge, the water got deeper and the swells larger. When we passed under the bridge, I reached out and grabbed one of the pilings that supported it and hung on. The boat crashed against the piling and stopped drifting.

We sat there as the boat beat rhythmically against the bridge. "Knock, knock," Rosie said.

"Knock-knock jokes? How lame."

"Better than just sitting here being scared."

I sighed and asked, "Who's there?"

"Canoe."

"Canoe who?"

"Canoe get us out of here?"

"Very funny," I said, and the wind rose.

"Do you think we'll freeze or starve to death first? And will they have to pry your dead hand off the piling with a crowbar?"

"Cut it out, Rosie. I heard once about a shark jumping right into a boat. What if a shark—"

"I don't care as long as it's not a seagull."

"Well, then, what if gulls find us and—"

"Knock, knock," said Rosie again.

"Who's there?"

"Lettuce."

"Lettuce who?"

"Lettuce not talk about scary things anymore."

I groaned, but actually Rosie was funny and smart and friendly. If we lived through this, we could probably be friends even though she was a Fribble.

There was silence but for the water lapping at the boat and the boat beating against the bridge. My arm grew tired from holding on. "Do you think we could switch places without tipping us over so you can take a turn?"

Rosie was scuttling over to my side when we heard the sound of a small outboard motor. "Millie, someone's coming!

We're saved!" Rosie jumped up and waved. "Here! Over here!"

The boat *putt-putt*ed nearer.

"How absotively mortifying to have to be rescued," I said. "Yikes! It's Rocky!" I threw myself into the bottom of the boat, and Rosie had to scramble to grab the piling. "Does he have his pants on yet?" I mumbled.

"Yes, and even a shirt. You should be talking to him. You know him."

"I can't. No matter what, I can't. I'd rather drown."

Rocky's boat pulled closer. "Have a problem?"

"The oar thing broke," said Rosie, "and we're drifting out to sea."

Rocky threw her a rope. "Tie this to the hook in the bow and I'll tow you back in."

Rosie did. "We were getting awful cold and tired of holding on to this bridge. You're a lifesaver, Rocky."

"Do I know you?"

"Everyone on Mission Beach knows you, Rocky," Rosie said with a grin.

I pinched her leg. "Stop flirting with him."

"Why? Do you want to flirt with him? I can move so you—"

"Flirt? Are you kidding? I'm positively expiring from embarrassment here!" While Rocky slowly towed us, I huddled in the bottom of the boat, popping my head out once in a while to see if we were back yet. Finally Rocky pulled close to the bay-side beach and swung the rowboat right onto the mudflats. Rosie called out, "Bye, Rocky, and thank you again."

"You're welcome, you and your little friend there in the bottom of the boat."

Rosie snorted, and I grunted, "Little???" but I stayed hidden until the *putt-putt* of the motor faded away.

"He's cute. You like him?" Rosie asked.

My cheeks grew hot. "He's old, and I mostly hate boys anyway."

"Wait until you're fourteen like me. I find there's a lot to be said for boys who aren't Leo or Dicky or Dwayne. You'll see."

"I'll wait," I said.

Rosie helped me pull the boat onto the sand, high enough so the incoming tide would not take it. And she went home to the Fribbles, dragging her feet all the way. Who could blame her?

After dinner Lily and Pete planned their costumes for Halloween on Friday. Pete, of course, would be the Lone Ranger. "I'm the daring and resourceful masked rider of the plains," he shouted. *Bang! Bang! Bang!* "The Lone Ranger rides again!"

"I want to be whatever you are, Millie," said Lily.

I pulled a sheet over my head.

"You're going to be a ghost?" Lily asked.

"No, I'm dressing like this whenever I go out for the rest of my life."

NOVEMBER 2, 1941
SUNDAY

I was huddled in the bottom of the boat with but one oar-lock for a quiet moment with *The Secret Garden*. Grumpy, gloomy Mary Lennox reminded me of me, and Colin was a drip like Lily until he got healthy and nice.

Far too soon, Pete found me. Leaning over, he said, "There you are. We want to march on Mission Boulevard but Mama won't say yes unless you come with us and we pull a wagon for when Lily gets tired." Mission Boulevard ran right down the middle of the spit called Mission Beach, ocean on one side, bay on the other. What stores and bars and eating places Mission Beach had were there. Pete and a pack of kids had been marching up and down in front of our house, shouting against Hitler while watching for German ships through their toilet-paper-tube binoculars, but it seemed they wanted to expand their area of operations.

"Go peddle your papers elsewhere, Jackson," I said. "I'm busy."

"What does that mean?"

"It means beat it, get lost, scram."

"Mama said."

Leaping from the boat, I headed for the house, calling, "Moth-errrr!"

Mama waved me off. "Your father is working and I have to go downtown. Mission Boulevard won't be safe for the little ones alone with so many strangers about. You are in charge of the group." She dropped a quarter and a dime into my hand. "Here, buy burgers for the three of you. No keeping the change this time, and don't let the kids get into any trouble."

So I had to accompany the motley troops up Bayside Walk and over to Mission Boulevard. Gram would have approved of them marching against Nazis and war, but there were unfortunately way too many opportunities for people to see me and laugh.

"Why are you wearing Pop's fishing hat pulled down like that?" Lily asked me as we gathered.

"Never mind." I tilted my head up and peered from under the brim. "Let's get this show on the road."

Artie and Archie, nine-year-old twins from up the beach, led the parade, waving homemade *Down with Hitler* signs. In purple crayon. The twins were exactly alike—blond hair, pug noses, missing front teeth—except that Archie's gut troubled him and he burped and hiccuped frequently and loudly, kind of like Cousin Edna but without the Jungle Gardenia. Behind were Lily, who shouldered a broom like a rifle, and Pete, with his cap pistols bouncing against his thighs. Then came MeToo, waggling his loose front tooth with his fingers as he walked, and Ralphie, pulling his Radio Flyer wagon, without Pepperoni, who was ailing. I hung back far enough so no one would see me with them.

As we marched up Bayside Walk, Artie began to chant: *"Hitler, Hitler, I bet your brain couldn't be little-er."* Pretty clever. I'll bet Artie could earn more soup and soap flakes writing advertising jingles than Mama. She ought to sign him up.

"Stay at home, you nasty fellow, or I'll punch you 'til you bellow," sang Artie.

"Me too!" shouted MeToo.

Burp went Archie.

They all clapped and cheered. It's funny how little kids could sing songs and laugh about Hitler and it didn't scare them one bit. Even the sound of his name got me worrying. I shook my head. There were obviously some advantages to being five.

The parade turned on Dover to Mission Boulevard, passed the roller coaster at the amusement center, and marched on. The mild Sunday afternoon had drawn lots of people: families with kids and ice cream cones, gaggles of teen girls in swimsuits, and mobs of uniformed sailors with caps tilted just so over their foreheads, looking like the Sailor Jack figure on Cracker Jack boxes. Would I be adding some of their names to my book? I shook my head and plodded on with the little marchers.

One of the sailors called out, "Good for you, kiddies. Give them Jerries something to worry about!" and his companions cheered. Pete, Artie, and Ralphie saluted and chanted louder. MeToo waggled his tooth and Archie hiccuped. My cheeks grew hot, and I pulled my hat down lower. *Can you die of embarrassment?* I wondered as I stumbled into a lamppost.

Spider Grossman was leaning against the front of his tattoo parlor at the corner of Mission and Ventura. "What're ya squirts doin'?" he called. I peeked from beneath my hat. Spider was dressed, as usual, in an aloha shirt, swim trunks, and sandals. It was almost a uniform. If it ever snowed in San Diego, Spider would still be in an aloha shirt, swim trunks, and sandals.

"We're marching against Hitler," Artie shouted, and the others cheered. "He can't come here and push us around. I'd pound him."

"Me too," said MeToo.

"Wanna march with us?" Pete asked.

"Naw. You don't get me joinin' nuthin'." Spider went back into his shop to ink an anchor on another sailor's arm.

Icky Fribble's brother, Dwayne, and his gang of hoodlums tumbled out of the Beach Club Bar. Stumbling and shouting, they laughed and hooted. "What's this, the Rose Parade?" one asked. Dwayne called, "Watch out, Hitler. The McGargles are after you!" And they lurched after us, laughing and jeering.

I could happily have added Dwayne to my Book of Dead Things, but there he was, swaggering and alive and loathsome as ever. "Plans have changed," I told my crew. "We're going home. Now." I hustled them back to the bay side and turned south, but Dwayne and his pals still followed.

Dwayne came right up behind me, belching beer breath.

"Dicky tells me you have a German spy in your house. A black-haired spy who talks Kraut. People around here wouldn't like that if they knew."

"Spy? Baloney!" I said. "Icky is a blockhead. And so are you." I may be afraid of war, death, and being poor, but I was not afraid of a weaselly bully like Dwayne Fribble.

"And that crazy granny of yours with her pickets and petitions. She was downright un-American."

"Don't call my gram crazy," said Lily, and she smacked Dwayne in the knee with the handle of her broom.

I snatched Lily before Dwayne could and dropped her into the wagon. Grabbing Pete's hand, I shouted, "This way, marchers," and tore back down Bayside Walk toward home.

"We haven't finished marching," Pete said, panting beside me.

"We are most definitely finished. We're going home and staying there."

"Me too!" shouted MeToo.

"Is Cousin Edna really a spy?" Pete asked.

"Nah, that's a bunch of hooey."

Fourteen feet slapped against the path, and wagon wheels squealed. *"Down with Hitler!"* shouted Artie and Pete. *"Form a posse and nab a Nazi!"*

"Hic," said Archie.

"I'm getting carsick," said Lily in the wagon.

No one was home but for Cousin Edna in the kitchen frying Spam for a sandwich. I sent the others away and put a tired Lily and Pete down for naps in the big bed, promising them hamburgers when they woke.

"Tell us a story," said Lily.

"Please," added Pete.

"Okay, a quick one. Once there was an awful Nazi villain named Hitler, and when he heard that Lily and Pete McGonigle were marching against him, he got so scared that he jumped in the river and drowned."

"With his boots on?" asked Pete.

"Did all the Nazis follow him?" Lily wanted to know.

"That's all I got, kids. Make up the rest yourselves." I returned to the kitchen.

"*Wie geht's?* What's up?" asked Edna, swaying to Glenn Miller playing "Elmer's Tune" from the radio.

"Edna, stop! You have to quit spouting German like that. It isn't safe. People are talking about you, calling you a spy."

"Poppycock!" said Edna. "I'm no spy, but I do like German fellows. So good-looking with their mustaches! Even Hitler." She spread mustard on bread and added the Spam. She took a bite and grease dribbled down her chin.

"Hitler? He's a monster, a wolf, eating up one country after another."

"I can't believe he's doing what they say he is doing. Such a *nett Gesicht,* a nice face. Maybe it's all a mistake."

"For crying out loud, you talk crazy like that and you'll get us all in trouble." My heart pounded.

Glenn Miller was finished and it was time for the news: *"We have more about the sinking of the American destroyer USS* Reuben James *by a German submarine. One hundred fifteen crew members are lost and presumed dead."*

"Such a nice face, huh, Edna?" I shouted, my belly

cramped and my voice louder than I intended. "See what your handsome Hitler has done now."

Edna shook her head. *"Nein, nein,"* she said. It may have been German, but I knew what she was saying. "It's a mistake, I'm sure. Wait and see."

NOVEMBER 9, 1941
SUNDAY

It was seventy-five degrees and sunny, and the tide was out. I pulled on my bathing suit and slogged through the mud-flats to the water. Bay water was warmer than seawater but still so cold I had to inch my way in. Finally I ducked under, shivered, and swam out.

There were no other swimmers in the bay. Well, no other human swimmers. I saw a seal, head up and staring at me, his whiskers twitching. When I swam a bit, so did he. When I stopped, so did he. When I ducked into the water, he ducked.

I was swimming with a seal! That was the magic of the bay. Some people prefer the Plunge at the amusement center. It's Mission Beach's claim to fame: the largest indoor heated pool in Southern California. But you can't see seals or hear gulls or watch sand dollars sway at the Plunge.

Gram once heard that brown and black people weren't welcome to swim there, and she blew her top. She said, "Your grandpa Harry and I had a hard time finding jobs and houses because we were Irish. People shoved and spit at us, and landlords and shopkeepers posted signs saying *No Dogs or. Irish."* Ever after, she wouldn't stand for people treating anyone the way she'd been treated. Gram marched and picketed and signed petitions. And just in case the rumors were true, she boycotted the Plunge. And I boycotted the Plunge because Gram did.

I floated gently, thinking of Gram. Why did she die when I needed her? How could she just leave me? If she were here today, we'd be eating red licorice and listening to Frank Sinatra and making pumpkin pies for Thanksgiving. *Macushla,* she'd call me, and she'd brush my hair a hundred strokes with her silver hairbrush. "Harry," she told me, "gave me this brush on our wedding day. And when I go to join him, it will be yours."

I fancied that brush, but when Gram died and the brush came to me, there was no joy in it. It sits unused in my underwear drawer. I'd a million times rather have Gram than a thousand thousand thousand silver brushes. I dived down in the water so you couldn't tell my tears from bay water.

The seal swam off, so I did, too. I'd left a shovel and a pail of water on the shore. I was going to dig for clams. That was another magical thing about the bay. You didn't have to go to the butcher or the market for everything. Things to eat were all around, in the water, the mud, the sand, even if most of them were perch.

Once Pop and I used to dig for clams together. We had so much fun. No fun today, but at least I could imagine Mama's surprise when I show up with clams for dinner without being told.

Clamming was hard work, but unlike abalone fishing, there was no risk of my being swept out to sea. I stuck the shovel into the mud over and over until I hit what felt like a rock. Then I dug furiously around it until I could grab the clam and drop it into the bucket. Phew. One. It was a good size, so only ten or so more and we'd have enough for clam fritters, if we have eggs. Or to mix with spaghetti, parsley, lemon, and a little butter, if we have butter. Yum. The very thought of settling for fried perch kept me digging until my arms ached and the scratchy, prickly feeling of the salt drying on my skin sent me home for lunch. I put the clams in a bucket with fresh water so they'd spit out any sand and we could eat them without grinding our teeth down.

"I have a bucket of clams outside, Mama," I said, washing the sand off my hands. "We could have them for dinner."

Handing me a sandwich, Mama said, "Fine, but your pop went fishing with Otto Lempke this morning and brought home a beautiful flounder. We'll eat it while it's fresh and have your clams tomorrow."

Christopher Columbus! Here I do something special to please Mama and that's all she says. *Fine.* Where's a hug and a *Thank you, Millie.* And flounder? Flat, flaky white fish. Just a big perch.

"I want you to spend some time with Lily," Mama said.

I nearly choked on my sandwich. "Why?"

"Because she's your sister."

"Isn't that punishment enough for me? Do I have to hang around with her, too? Rosie and I were going to look for—"

"Mildred McGonigle, shame on you. Lily loves you and looks up to you. Be nice to her. Take her for a walk. Build a sand castle. Play in the water. Be a big sister."

I opened my mouth to argue but Mama said, "Do it! Be

sure to watch over her and come right home if she gets cold or tired. And don't let her get sunburned. You know how pale and delicate she is."

I grabbed a towel and a book. Lily was waiting outside, in her bright green playsuit and sun hat, her yellow hair tied in two bunches over her ears. She was all smiley and eager and I might have thought she was cute if she were someone else's sister.

"Come on, you pill. If I have to do this, let's do it."

Lily picked up her little pail and shovel. She scurried to keep up with me. "Why don't you like me?"

"Because you're a pill."

"Pete's a pill sometimes and you like him."

"Pete's a lovable pill who doesn't whine and snivel."

Lily snuffled. "Am *I* not lovable?"

"C'mon, Lily. Mama loves you. She loves you best." I picked up a stone and skipped it into the water with all my might. "Isn't that enough?"

More snuffles from Lily. "No. I want *you* to like me, Millie."

I sighed. Holy cow. I guessed it wasn't her fault she was Mama's favorite. I took her hand. "I like you okay, Lily, most of the time. You're my little sister."

We were quiet then as we walked down to the jetty at the south end of the beach and around to the ocean side. "Let's stay here," Lily said. "I want to build a sand castle."

"Just do it silently. I want to read." The sun was high in the blue, blue sky. Lily set to work on her castle. I spread my towel on the sand. Melody Grayson down the beach was in college and she had lent me her copy of *The Yearling*. She said it was likely gloomy and depressing enough for me. There'd been no tragedy yet, but I had hopes. If somebody in the book died, could I add it to my Book of Dead Things? Why not? I make the rules.

"What are you reading, Millie?" Lily asked.

"*The Yearling*, about a boy and a deer."

"Tell me about it."

"Later. I'm reading."

The day went on. Lily fell asleep and I was immersed in the Florida backwoods and not Mission Beach. The further I got, the sadder, but I couldn't look away. By the time I finished, my face was wet with tears. How could Mr. Baxter shoot a deer? How could Mrs. Baxter do it? How could Jody lose the thing he loved most in the world and still go on?

I put the book down and stretched. I didn't know how much time had passed, but a cool breeze was rising. "Let's go home, Lily," I said.

She woke up and squealed. "*Ow, ow.* Millie, my face hurts. And my back. Look, Millie. *Ow. Ow.*"

Holy cow! Lily's nose, cheeks, and chin were bright red. And her shoulders!

"You let me get all burned up," Lily whimpered. "You're not a good sister."

Which was just what Mama said when we got home. I was blamed, of course, even though I said I was sorry but the sun wasn't my fault. I must admit when Lily cried as Mama put her in a cool-water bath to soothe her burns, I felt pretty bad. Maybe I could borrow a nickel from Mama for ice cream for Lily. I could work it off by . . . I shook my head. I didn't do anything worth a nickel.

Pop and Pete came back from wherever they'd been, sweaty and fishy-smelling. Lily told them all about her sunburn. They glared at me and patted Lily on an unburned part of her back. I was a social outcast in my own home.

There was a knock at the door. Maybe someone else to blame me for failing Lily. Maybe a reporter from the *San Diego Union* come to interview the girl who let her sister burn. Holy cow.

It wasn't. It was Mrs. Wagner, another former North Park neighbor.

"Come in," Pop said. "Sit yourself down. How are Howie and—"

"Fine, Martin, fine. Sorry to interrupt but I've come with a message from Billie Harlow." She pulled a handkerchief from her pocket and wiped at her nose. "Her son Garland has been hospitalized with infantile paralysis. Polio."

Pop muttered, "Oh, no," and Mama said, "Dear God!" and started to cry. I'd heard of polio but didn't really know what it meant, so I pulled on Pop's sleeve.

"It's a disease that attacks a person's nervous system," he said, patting my shoulder, "weakening the muscles."

"In Garland's case," Mrs. Wagner said, "he's too weak to breathe on his own. He's in an iron lung."

I shivered as Mrs. Wagner described the iron lung: "It's a tube-shaped metal machine that he lies in with only his head sticking out. Bellows pump air in and out, helping him to breathe." It sounded so creepy, like something from a horror movie.

"How does he go to the bathroom?" Pete asked.

Mama shushed him but Mrs. Wagner just smiled. "I'm

sure the doctors and nurses know the best ways to take care of him. Billie wanted all the families with children at Garland's party to know since polio is contagious in its early stages and your Pete was . . ." She nodded toward Pete, who asked, "Can I have an iron lung, too?"

"Quiet, Pete," Pop said. He lifted him up and hugged him.

Mama grabbed Lily. "Do you feel all right? Can you breathe? Are you feverish?" She felt Lily's forehead and looked in her eyes. "All you kids, let us know if you, well, if you feel, well, different."

Mrs. Wagner left to alarm some other family. Mama questioned us all about sore throats, coughing, and muscle aches. Pop poured a small glass of whiskey. Luckily for me, Lily's sunburn was forgotten in the face of bigger tragedy.

Before bed I went into the kitchen for a last glass of water. Soft sounds of whimpering came from the sofa. "Pete, honey, what's wrong?" I asked.

"I want to see Garland and give him the nickel I pinched from his birthday card."

"Good idea, but you'll have to wait until he's better."

Pete snuffled. "It's not long until Christmas, and Garland's in the hospital. How will Santa find him?"

Oh, Pete. What if Pete caught what Garland had? What if Pete got sick and had to breathe with an iron lung? What if I did? I grabbed him and held on tightly.

NOVEMBER 17, 1941
MONDAY

Lily recovered from her sunburn. Her skin blistered and peeled, and she and Pete had a contest about who could peel off the longest strand. Disgusting!

Mama still felt our foreheads and looked at our throats every day since Garland got sick. No polio was going to get past her into this house. But we all seemed healthy enough, even Lily, who wasn't as whiny as usual.

After school and a walk along the bay, sketching dead things in my book—a tiny sandpiper with a long thin bill, parts of a purple sea urchin, and an army of sand crabs—I found Mama in the kitchen, snuffling while she made a grocery list for Thanksgiving dinner. Tears spotted her face. "This will be my first Thanksgiving without my mother," Mama said. "I'll miss her terribly."

"Me too." I sat, elbows on the table. "Remember that time she forgot to turn on the oven and we had Thanksgiving dinner at midnight?"

"And when your pop taught her to float and she started

to float out into the middle of the bay and he had to swim out and tow her back."

"And how Disney cartoonists went on strike and she carried a petition to the amusement center and told people that Mickey and Goofy and Donald Duck were on strike, and little kids began crying and begging their parents to sign."

I didn't know if we were laughing or crying, but the kitchen was noisy with it. Lily and Pete, not wanting to miss anything, hurried in. "What's going on?"

"We're just remembering Gram and missing her," Mama said. "This will be our first Thanksgiving without her—and her oven. Ours isn't big enough for a turkey."

"What will we have, then?" I grimaced. "Perch?"

"Sure, I could stuff a perch."

Three faces fell. "I was just kidding," I said.

"So was I," said Mama. "How about a big chicken?"

"Or hot dogs," said Pete. "Or—"

"Cotton candy!" Lily cried.

Mama pulled Pete to her with one arm and Lily with the other. "A big chicken it is," said Mama. "With Gram's turkey stuffing but without her famous pecan pumpkin pie, I'm afraid."

Pop came home from the Burger Shack, waving a letter. "This came for you, Miss Millie," he said, lifting it high above my head. "Do you have a boyfriend we don't know about who's writing you love notes?" He winked.

Every time I reached for the letter, Pop held it higher. "The return address is in New Jersey. Who do you know in New Jersey?"

"Stop teasing her, Martin," Mama said, swatting him with a dish towel. "Give her the letter."

I tore it open. A letter . . . and a five-dollar bill! "I won a contest! For a jingle. I won five dollars!"

"Maybe it's a mistake," Pop said, his brow furrowed. "Maybe it's really for you, Lois."

I handed the letter to Mama. "No, it's for Mildred McGonigle," Mama said. "Did you send a jingle to the Campbell's soup people?"

"I did. I sent it in so long ago that I forgot all about it. Now it seems I won an honorable mention."

"I send in hundreds, and you win five dollars with your very first try," Mama said. Her voice sounded tired and sad. "I'm driving myself crazy with rhymes and jingles in my head. I dream in rhyme. My grocery list rhymes: *Do I need bread or sandwich buns? Piggly Wiggly, here I come.* I'm going nuts, and for what? Soap coupons and discounts on toilet paper!"

"Sorry, Mama."

She shook her head. "Just ignore me." She gave me a hug. "Congratulations! What's the winning jingle?"

"I was inspired by the time Edna lost her teeth on the beach and we had to sift sand all afternoon to find them."

"It was me!" Pete shouted. "I found them!"

"Yes, you did. And here's the jingle":

Campbell's Beef Broth, for a taste of meat
so light and smooth you won't need teeth.

Pop poured 7-Up all around. "Here's to our Millie," he said, "who inherited her mother's green eyes and poetic talent." We all clinked glasses while Pete shot off his cap guns: *Bang! Bang! Bang!*

The to-do woke Edna from a nap in the bedroom. She ran in, shouting, "*Wunderbar! Wunderbar!* What do we celebrate?"

"Five dollars!" Pop said. "See, Millie, cheer up. Life's not all doom and gloom."

I didn't know how to feel. What with winning a contest and earning so much money, I was pretty joyful. But merriment during sad and scary times seemed wrong somehow. Bombs were falling, people were dying, and I was feeling happy. It wasn't right. I needed to cheer *down*.

So the next morning I took myself over to Mission Boulevard, where between the real-estate office and the liquor store was the library.

"Mrs. Pennyfeather," I said to the librarian, "I want to read some sad books about danger and death. What does the library have like that?"

"Now, what do you need those for?"

"For my education," I said. Librarians and teachers are suckers for anything having to do with education.

Mrs. Pennyfeather pushed her glasses up on her head. "Well, *War and Peace* has lots of danger and death, I suppose, but I wouldn't call it a sad book. Not like *Grapes of Wrath* about the Depression and the Dust Bowl. That's pretty tragic. And *Of Mice and Men* is downright heartbreaking." She blinked a few times and sighed.

"Do plenty of sorrowful things happen? Do people die? Can I check them out?"

"They're adult books, Millie, in the adult section. You'll have to wait until you're thirteen."

"Are there books with dead people in the kiddie section?"

She frowned at me and shook her head. "Millie, Millie." I said nothing and she went on. "I can't think of any offhand. There are sad books—*The Velveteen Rabbit,* about a toy nobody wants anymore, or *Black Beauty,* about a horse mistreated and separated from those who love him. There is sadness and suffering but they end on a happier note."

"I don't want a happier note. This is not a cheery time. What's the saddest children's book about death you ever read that didn't end happily?"

Mrs. P eyed me uncertainly. "I'd rather give you something light and merry. Like *The Saturdays* or *The Peterkin Papers.* Playing the piano through the window!" She chuckled. "I loved the Peterkins when I was a girl."

In the Dark Ages, I thought. I shook my head.

"Well, then, how about *The Moffats.* That's pretty funny."

The Moffats? Did she think I was six? "No, thanks, Mrs. P. Maybe I'll read *Little Women* again. The part where Beth dies."

I stomped my way home.

NOVEMBER 23, 1941
SUNDAY

Mama and Lily had gone to take a tuna casserole and brownies to old Mrs. Dunsmore, a neighbor who had broken her leg. Pop was working at the Burger Shack. Pete was at Ralphie's birthday party, and Edna lay outside in the sunshine. I was alone in the house, enjoying the silence, eating peanut butter on saltines. I was looking through the Sears catalog, wondering how to spend my five-dollar prize money, when a wailing Pete hurled himself onto my lap. His loud gurgling sobs sounded like the sink backing up. I patted his back and waited, my stomach tight and my heart pounding. Was he sick? Was it polio? Or was the war here? Had the Germans invaded?

"The Lone Ranger," he finally squeezed out. "Ralphie said . . . said the Lone Ranger . . ." There were more sobs.

The knot of worry in my belly loosened. "Ralphie said what?"

"Said the Lone Ranger is dead! Dead! You can have him for your dead book and I don't care! I hate the Lone Ranger!"

"Oh, Petey, that happened a long time ago. But it was the actor who played the Lone Ranger on radio who died. Now they have a new one."

"No! Ralphie said it was the real Lone Ranger and he's dead and every other Lone Ranger is fake!" I didn't tell Pete that Tom Mix was also dead. A five-and-a-half-year-old can only take so much bad news.

"Why do you listen to Ralphie, Pete? Didn't he tell you that in the next *Tom and Jerry* cartoon, Tom would catch and eat Jerry?"

"Yes."

"Was that true?"

"No."

"Didn't Ralphie say if you eat watermelon seeds and dirt, a melon will grow in your belly and you'll be full of watermelon all the time?"

"Yeah."

"And was that true?"

"No."

"So why do you believe Ralphie now?"

"Because it's true." He wiped his nose on his sleeve. "I just know it."

"Go back to Ralphie's party, Pete, and don't worry. They'll get another actor and—"

"No! No more Lone Ranger! He's dead! I loved the Lone Ranger and now I hate the Lone Ranger!" Pete jumped from my lap, ripped off his gun belt, and threw it on the floor. "Here, draw this in your book." And he ran into the bedroom.

Poor Petey. He seemed more angry than sad. But it wasn't fair to be angry with someone for dying, was it? Was it?

Pete knowing about my book felt wrong, but I didn't know why. I chewed on my lip in thought for a moment but then busied myself adding *Actor who played Lone Ranger* to my Book of Dead Things. I couldn't remember his name, but it seemed a way to honor Pete's grief.

There came a series of loud hiccups at the front door.

"Petey," I called, "Archie's here."

"Don't care."

Obviously Pete needed a new hero or he wouldn't be himself again, and I had an idea where to find one. I pulled on a sweater. "I have to go out for a minute," I called. "Edna is right outside if you need anything."

"Don't care."

I bumped into Archie at the door. "Where's Artie? I never see you without him."

"Artie is tied to a tree by bandits, waiting for the Lone Ranger to come rescue him."

"Well, the Lone Ranger is indisposed at the moment."

"What's that mean?"

"It means you'll have to save Artie yourself today."

Archie left with a final *hic*.

I headed to Bell's Grocery. There was a blue star in the store window—I'd heard that Walter, the oldest Bell boy, had joined the navy—and several posters urging folks to give to Polish War Relief and Greek War Relief and French War Relief. It seemed as if all of Europe needed relief, and Mr. Bell was determined that they get it.

Bell's was not open on Sundays, but the Bell family lived behind. I found Mr. Bell sitting outside, reading his newspaper. "Sorry," he said when he saw me. "All the movie-star magazines are locked inside today. Something else I can do for you?"

I explained my mission and Mr. Bell handed over the comic section. Then, holding up the front page, he said, "Says here Hitler has a peace plan. Maybe things'll turn out okay after all. I mean, no one wants war. Even Hitler, it seems."

At home again, I sat on the sofa and searched through the comics for a new hero for Pete. Red Ryder? No. That would mean more cap guns and more *bang! bang! bang!* Dick Tracy? Same thing. I paused to read *Popeye* and *Nancy,* and then there it was: *Buck Rogers in the 25th Century.* Perfect.

Rattling the newspaper loudly and often, I shouted *"Wow!"* and *"Oh boy!"* and *"You tell 'em!"* It wasn't long before Pete came snuffling out of the bedroom. "What're you doing?"

"I'm reading the funnies from the Sunday paper. *Buck Rogers in the 25th Century.*"

"What's that?"

"Oh, it's the best. Buck Rogers is a hero fighting evil spacemen and that blackhearted bum Killer Kane. The whole fate of the world—the universe even—depends on him."

Pete climbed onto my lap and I read Buck's adventures aloud.

"Are there bathrooms in spaceships?" Pete asked.

"I guess."

"How do they go pee-pee with those space suits on?"

"I don't know. Maybe they're hooked up with tubes and wires, or maybe they just pee in their suits."

"Neat! I might—"

"Don't you dare."

Pete grinned. "What if they are wearing space helmets and they have to throw up?"

"Gross, Pete, enough. How should I know?" Pete was silent while he thought of another annoying question, so I hurried on. "Archie was here a while ago. Artie has been tied to a tree by evil spacemen and he needs help."

"Really?" Pete jumped off my lap. "Hold on, Artie," he hollered. "I'll save you." He grabbed his cap pistols and ran to the door. *Bang! Bang! Bang!* "I am Buck Rogers of the twenty-fifth century!"

"Wait a minute, there, Buck. Heroes in the twenty-fifth century have ray guns, which shoot super-silent light rays: *whoosh whoosh whoosh.*"

"Yeah?"

"Yeah. Let me hear those ray guns."

"Whoosh! Whoosh!" he shouted.

"Even more silent."

"Whoosh," Pete whispered, and he was off.

I smiled. Pete was happy again. He sure was quick to bounce back. The house would be quieter now that he was Buck Rogers, and the Lone Ranger and his six-shooters were gone. Planes thundered overhead, and I shuddered. Life was much easier when you were five and a half.

"Mama," I asked as I set the table for dinner, "do you think Mrs. Dunsmore will die?"

"No, she's healing nicely."

"Well, do we know anyone who died recently or is about to?"

"How morbid. Why do you ask?"

"I want to know more names of dead people."

"Millie, you are the most peculiar child."

Me, peculiar? Mama should have a talk with Pete sometime.

NOVEMBER 29, 1941
SATURDAY

"**M**y mother wants you to come to dinner," I told Rosie.
"I'd love to."

"You won't say that after. It's likely to be a circus."

"Listen, it means I'll miss dinner at the Fribbles', which is like a bad horror movie. *Dinner at the Fribbles',*" Rosie boomed, "*with King Kong as Dwayne Fribble, Frankenstein as Dicky Fribble, and starring the Wicked Witch of the West as Mrs. Bertha Fribble. There will be action-packed terror and violence and gross stupidity and more. . . .* I'd prefer a circus any day."

So it was on. Rosie arrived at five o'clock exactly, carrying a sprig of white-blossomed sage in a 7-Up bottle. The piney, sharp scent of the sage filled the room.

"How sweet, Rosie," Mama said, and she took a big sniff before shutting it in the refrigerator. Lily, of course, was allergic.

Edna, Pop, and Lily were already sitting at the table, and Rosie joined them. "I want to sit next to Rosie," Pete said, and he grabbed an empty chair and shoved it between Edna and Rosie. It was not a promising start.

As we owned only six chairs, I had to sit on a pile of sofa pillows and rest my chin on the table.

Pete screeched, "Eeeek! It's the Evil Body-less Head come to destroy the earth. Prepare for your doom! *Mwah-ha-ha!*"

"Pete, behave," said Mama.

"You do look awful funny that way, Millie," said Lily. "Big head and no body." She pointed at me and grinned. "Hey, I know where the Headless Horseman can find a head."

"Knock it off, Lily, or you can sit down here."

"Consider it your throne, Millie, my princess," said Pop. "Your perch." He slapped his knee. "Perch, Millie! Perch! Get it?"

"I waaant a throne, too," Lily whined. "But not perch."

Pete pounded the table in frantic laughter. "Millie's sitting on a big fish! Does it stink like fish guts?"

"Don't be crude, Pete," Mama called from the kitchen. "And, Martin, you either."

Pop winked. "I'm in trouble now."

Rosie and I looked at each other. Her face was red and sort of scrunched up. Was she disgusted by us? Ready to run off? Would I lose a friend?

"Enough of this babbling," Pop said. "Rosie, how do you like living here at the beach?"

"It's nice. I like it mostly." Her lips were thin and her voice tight, so unlike Rosie. Was she shy?

Before Rosie could say anything more, Mama brought in platters and bowls of fried chicken, mashed potatoes, and canned peas, and we helped ourselves.

Pete held up a chicken wing and asked, "Is this squirrel? Sure looks like squirrel."

"Squirrel? Not squirrel!" And Lily started to blubber.

With his mouth full, Pete said, "Best squirrel I ever ate."

"Enough, Pete. It's not squirrel," Mama said.

"I'd like more squirrel," said Pop with a grin.

Lily squealed.

"Martin, quit fooling around. Honestly, you're as bad as Pete," Mama said, her mouth pinched. "You, Lily, stop crying. You know they're teasing. Pete, find something else to talk about besides squirrel. And everyone stop acting like ninnies. We have a guest."

"Willa Silver can play the ukulele with her feet. And Waldo Swelter's feet stink so bad you can smell him coming."

Rosie squirmed and clamped her lips shut.

Mama closed her eyes. "Thank you, Pete. Enough about feet. Anyone else?"

"Speaking of squirrel," Edna said, and Mama groaned. "On the farm we ate squirrel and possum. What's the big deal? When you're hungry, you eat what's there."

Mama sighed. "Edna, dear, you've never lived on a farm."

"I'm sure I did. I remember getting up at five to milk the cows, haul logs, drag in ice from the pond for the icebox—"

"Wait a minute," I shouted. "I know that story. That's Laura Ingalls Wilder's *Farmer Boy*."

Edna frowned. "No."

"Remember, it's all about her husband, Almanzo, when he was a boy. You must have read it sometime."

"Almanzo, yes. He was there, too. Good-looking boy."

"Can we have possum instead of squirrel next time?" Pete asked, then added, "What's possum?"

"No possum!" cried Lily. "And no squirrel!" She pushed her plate away, and it smashed onto the floor.

That did it. The circus was in town. I looked at Rosie. I dreaded what I'd see there but she exploded into laughter, spraying a mouthful of canned peas across the table right onto Pop.

I excused myself and crawled into the bedroom to hide under the covers. Rosie must feel mortified. Between her eruption and the McGonigles' bad behavior, she'd never speak to me again.

"Where are you, Millie?" Rosie asked from the doorway. "I'm sorry if I embarrassed you. I couldn't help it. Everything was just so funny and I couldn't hold it in any longer."

I poked my head out. "Funny? *Funny?* You don't think we're weird and gross and crazy?"

"We're all a little crazy. And it was a whole lot better than *Dinner at the Fribbles'.*" She sat on the bed. "I like your family. No one's mean." She sighed. "Your pop reminds me a little of my dad. I miss him. This was a bit like being home with my family."

A loud crash came from the dining room. Rosie and I rushed in to see Pete and his chair sprawled on the ground. "I'm okay. Things look funny from down here. Come see."

"Get up here and finish your squirrel," Pop said.

"Martin!" From Mama.

Rosie smiled. "Maybe your family is a little louder and weirder."

"Absotively!" I took a deep breath of relief. Dinner at the McGonigles' was over and Rosie and I were still friends.

NOVEMBER 30, 1941
SUNDAY

A series of explosions woke me before dawn. With my heart tumbling wildly, I tore into Mama and Pop's room and jumped onto the bed, between them. "Is it war? Are the Germans here? What should we do?"

"Shh, Millie. It's okay." Pop smoothed my hair. "It's only big guns test-firing from the beach palisades in Point Loma. They're making sure everyone and everything is ready, just in case."

Lily slept through the noise but Pete, rubbing his eyes, joined us. "Is it Fourth of July? Can we have firecrackers, too?"

Pop picked Pete up and carried him, upside down and giggling, into the kitchen. Mama made pancakes for breakfast, but it was a gloomy affair. The pancakes were plain and round—no pancake hearts or smiles or cat faces with raisins for eyes. Pop used to get a newspaper and he'd read the comics aloud in funny voices while we ate our fancy pancakes. Now Mama thought the newspaper was a frill and we should save the five cents. And the radio was always on.

"Increasing Pacific tensions," a newsman shouted. *"A special Japanese envoy has arrived for what appears to be one more—possibly the last—joint effort to discover a formula for peace in the Pacific."*

My face and hands grew cold. "Japan? Do I have to worry about Japan, too?"

Mama turned the radio off. "Lily and Pete, go into the bedroom and play something. Edna, sit down. We grown-ups need to talk."

Lily stuck out her lower lip. "Millie's not a grown-up."

"For this conversation, she's close enough."

Pop settled Lily and Pete in the bedroom with paper and crayons and closed the door.

"You've heard the news," Mama said. "President Roosevelt says the U.S. may be at war in a year."

Edna harrumphed. "The United States should stay out of foreign wars. Hitler won't come here, and we shouldn't go there. It's all just talk."

Pop slammed his hand on the table. "Stop it, Edna! Every day we hear more about Nazi atrocities. Countries invaded and their residents slaughtered, Jews massacred, Jewish children—children!—murdered." He took a deep breath. "And it's not just Germany to fear. Despite Japanese envoys and peace offers, they may just be stalling while they get ready to attack. War is coming here. If not today, someday soon." He stuck his unlit pipe in his mouth.

My face grew cold. Pop was scaring me more than the explosions.

"Hitler may be as bad as they tell us," Edna said. "I don't know, but I know he won't come here. Why would he?

What have we done to him?" And with that she went to take a bath.

His teeth clenched around the stem of his pipe, Pop asked, "How does she know? Did he send her a telegram?"

"Martin, be serious," said Mama.

Pop grunted. "Millie, I won't tell you kids not to worry," he said, "but if war comes, San Diego is ready. The navy has installed powerful new guns and mortars and mined the harbor. Fort Rosecrans has been reinforced and thousands of artillery men trained. And you know I would never let anything bad happen to you guys."

I nodded, but I wished I could believe that. What could Pop do against Hitler and Nazis or invading Japanese?

There was a sharp knock on the door and Mrs. Fribble came screeching in. "I just saw Tilda Morris at church. She has it on good authority that the guns this morning mean the Germans have invaded! And she saw people at the butcher in Pacific Beach yesterday ordering bratwurst and whispering in German." Mrs. Fribble took a deep breath. "It's an invasion!"

"Easy, Bertha. The guns were fired for a readiness test," said Pop.

"That's what they tell us. How can we believe them, Roosevelt and his lousy Democrats! I tell you, Tilda Morris is right. It's an invasion!" Mrs. Fribble grabbed a cold pancake from the table and chewed. "The Germans have already planted spies everywhere. Gloria Mergaser said she heard from Aldus Topper at the filling station that they've trained dogs to bark in German to pass messages."

Mama swallowed a laugh and Pop drew strongly on his unlit pipe. "Now, Bertha—"

"Don't *Now, Bertha* me, Martin McGonigle. There are German spies right here in Mission Beach. I've seen reflections off binoculars and strange flashing lights. And now we've been invaded!"

Edna, greasy green beauty cream smeared on her face, scurried in from the bathroom. "*Mein Gott,* invaded?" she shouted. "For real? *Ach, mein Gott! Verdammt!*"

Mrs. Fribble stared at Edna, squeaked loudly, and tore out of the house.

Mama finally let her laugh loose. "I imagine she's off to spread sweetness and light at another lucky home."

"It's not funny, Mama," I said. "If Edna keeps talking German and defending Hitler, there'll be trouble."

"Millie's right," said Pop. "You'd better watch out, Edna. I'll bet Bertha Fribble turns you in to the FBI: *I tell you, Officer, there's a German spy with a green face! Right there in the McGonigles' house!*"

"*Phoof!*" said Edna, and she went back into the bathroom.

I pulled a jacket from the closet. "I'm going for a walk." I needed to be by myself to think about the war news Mama and Pop had shared. I walked over to the ocean side of Mission Beach. The sky was clear and wide, the wind pulled at my clothes, and the noise and fury of the crashing waves echoed the disquiet within me.

The sand was strewn with kelp, brown and shiny and reeking of the sea. I dragged a strand behind me, popping the gas-filled bubbles that kept it afloat in the ocean. The pops sounded like bullets, I imagined, though I'd never heard a bullet and hoped I never would.

A brown pelican soared overhead. Suddenly he folded his wings and, his beak like a spear, plunged into the water. With a great splash, he then shot up into the air with a fish in his bill. Gulls followed, squawking, in case he dropped the fish, but he tossed it up as he flew and caught it so that it slithered down his gullet. Would America be like that poor fish attacked from the air and swallowed whole? I snorted. *A little dramatic, McGonigle,* I thought. Mrs. Gillicuddy would say *Overwrought* and *Excessive* and make me rewrite.

I stood looking west. There was nothing but water between me and Japan. What were they doing over there right now? Were they mounting big guns and mortars and reinforcing their forts like we Americans were? Was a Japanese girl, worried and afraid, standing on the shore staring across the same water toward me at that very moment?

I didn't think I was like Mrs. Fribble, jumping at every noise and seeing spies in every bush, but I was plenty worried. That didn't make me a coward, did it? Other people were worried, too. Normal people, not like Mrs. Fribble. It seemed the cloud over my head had grown until now it covered most everyone in the country.

I'd been keeping the Book of Dead Things like Gram wanted me to. And signing it with McGonigle in the mud. We were all safe so far. Was that because of the book? Gram would likely know, but Gram was gone, and anyway, whatever she knew didn't keep *her* safe.

I walked down to the far end of the beach, my footsteps in the sand following behind me. After the mild Sunday, the sand was strewn here and there with what visitors had left behind—ruins of sand castles, bottle caps, cigarette butts. A jellyfish had washed ashore and lay stranded on the sand. But the tide would come in, leaving the beach clean and new when it ebbed again. I wished the whole world were like that. Bad things might happen, but just a turn of the moon and all would be well again.

DECEMBER 6, 1941
SATURDAY

"I have a quarter," Rosie said. "Let's go get Cokes and fries."

"Race you to the Shack."

"No, not the Burger Shack again. Let's do something different. Have an adventure."

"Like?"

"Like going to the soda fountain at Dunaway's. We'll walk and talk our heads off."

"That's in Pacific Beach. It'll take a long time."

"What else do you have to do?"

I shrugged and we set off.

"What's up with you?" Rosie asked. "Anything interesting going on at the McGonigles'? Any more squirrel dinners?"

I ignored that. "Pop is glued to the radio. Lots of scary news about Japan. And I'm just all filled up with worry—"

"Hold it right there. We're off to have an adventure. A fun adventure. Tell me gossip. Tell me stories. Tell me rumors. Just don't tell me the news."

So I told her about Skinny Pickens getting kicked out

of school for letting frogs loose in the first-grade classroom. And Ned Baxter setting off firecrackers in the teachers' lounge. Miss Warren, the kindergarten teacher, swooned and had to be carried to safety by Mr. Wilder, the assistant principal, and now they're engaged.

And Rosie told me about Mary Margaret Oglesby going steady with Frank Burnside and Leon Martins at the same time.

"How can she do that?"

"The bigger question is who on earth would want to go steady with Frank Burnside or Leon Martins?"

"Mary Margaret Oglesby," we said at the same time.

"I don't have any more gossip but I know a joke," I said. "A strawberry tried to cross the road and there was a traffic jam."

Rosie chuckled. "That's okay, but listen to this. It's my favorite joke." She cleared her throat and said: "A Roman soldier walks into a bar and holds up two fingers. 'Give me five Cokes,' he said." She grinned a big grin.

"So? What's the joke?"

Rosie held up her hand and made a V shape with two fingers. "See? Vee? Like the Roman numeral five. Get with it, Mil."

"I guess it's funny, but confusing if you don't know about Roman numerals. And I don't." I was a little annoyed. Was Rosie showing off? "Why, I could tell you a joke about sculpin and you wouldn't know what I was talking about."

"What's sculpin?"

"See!"

More bickering and gossip and bad jokes later, we finally

reached the drugstore. We grabbed two stools at the counter, sat and twirled and swung our feet. We blew the wrappers off the straws and ogled the soda jerk.

"Yowza," Rosie said, and whistled softly. "With those muscles he must lift a lot more than just ice cream cones."

"It's Buzz Pittman," I told her. "Bitsy Pittman's older brother. Bitsy says he lifts weights in front of a mirror so he can admire his muscles."

Someone dropped a nickel into the jukebox and the Sons of the Pioneers sang "Cool Water." Why the song was popular, I don't know. All about thirsty cowboys in the desert yearning for water.

Buzz brought our Cokes. "It's that dumb song again. I hate it! I hate stupid cowpokes and their stupid yodel singing." He raised his voice. "Who keeps playing that dumb song?" he asked, but no one answered.

We slurped our Cokes noisily and wiped our lips.

Buzz started to whip up a chocolate milkshake for some lucky person. "He's definitely cute," Rosie said, watching him.

"Phooey. Buzz is mean and a bully, and he's cute enough to get away with it." I blew a straw wrapper in his direction. "Like Dwayne and Icky, except for the cute part. Do they ever give you trouble?"

"I'd like to see them try. I couldn't win in a fistfight, but I can outrun and outthink them any day. Besides, they're pretty much cowards and like to pick on littler kids." Rosie put two nickels on the counter for our Cokes.

"Let's go," she said, and jumped off her stool. "But first . . ."

She crossed to the jukebox and put her last three nickels in. "This is dedicated to Buzz Pittman. Enjoy," she announced as she pressed C-7 three times: "Cool Water" by the Sons of the Pioneers. And we left,

"Whew, it's warm out here," Rosie said. She took off her sweater and fanned herself with it. "It's already snowing in Chicago." She laughed. "My brother's in trouble again. Leo was throwing snowballs to knock the hats off men getting off the streetcar. Unfortunately one of the men was our father."

"Sounds like he's as dumb as Icky," I said. We passed a bus stop, and I let out a deep breath. "No more nickels for the bus, I guess. We'll have to walk all the way back home."

Rosie smiled. "It's worth it," and we began to sing "Cool Water."

DECEMBER 7, 1941
SUNDAY

It was sunny and warm for December, seventy-six degrees a few minutes before noon. I'd worn my bathing suit all day but was not out in the water. Instead I was trapped inside doing homework. Edna had gone to the movies but I couldn't go with her. Bah, homework.

I was spread out on the bed trying to determine the area and circumference of given shapes. I hated area and circumference. Who cared? Mama was in the kitchen, listening to some old people's music and writing jingles, and Pop and Lily and Pete had gone for burgers. Mama and Pop were determined to keep us cheery and untroubled. We were going to eat lunch outside, splash in the water, skip stones, and pretend we weren't worried about war and the world. And tonight we were going to join the Fribbles for a bonfire and a sing-along. The Fribbles! For cryin' out loud, could this day get any worse? At least Rosie would be there, so we could—

"Millie!" a voice screamed from the other room.

My mother? Raising her voice?

"Millie!!!"

Good gravy. Don't flip your wig, Mama.

Mama pushed the bedroom door open and clutched my arm. "Run and find your father and the children. Now, Millie! Now!"

"What for? Why me? I have homework." I was getting a good whine going when Mama grabbed my shoulder and shook.

"The radio," Mama said. "The Japanese." She was breathing heavily. "Bombed the naval base at Pearl Harbor. In Hawaii. Sneak attack. Get your father now!"

I went. All I knew of Hawaii was pineapples and grass skirts, but it's part of the United States and close to home, not far away like Germany and France. Did Japanese bombs mean war really was coming here to Mission Beach? My throat was dry and my heart flopped like a fish as I ran. I met Pop and the kids coming home.

"Bombs," I said through pants and wheezes. "Hawaii. Bombs."

Pop handed me the sack of burgers, picked Lily up, and ran.

"What's happening?" Pete asked.

"The Japanese bombed Pearl Harbor," I told him.

"Who's Pearl Harbor?" Oh, how I wished I were only five and a half! I grabbed his hand and we ran together.

At home we all gathered by the radio. Even Edna, for the movie was called off after the attack was announced. I huddled on the sofa with Lily and Pete, who were wary and silent, their eyes puzzled, while Mama stood in the doorway, wringing her apron in her hands. Pop sat right in front of the radio and leaned forward, his forearms on his thighs, as though he could actually see what was happening if he got close enough.

He blew his nose with a hoot and muttered over and over, "The dirty so-and-sos." Tears streamed down his face. I had never seen him cry before, and it frightened me. I chewed on my cuticles until they bled.

Lily climbed onto Pop's lap and touched a tear running down his face. "Why you crying, Pop?"

"Grown-up stuff, Lily-billy. Nothing for you kids to worry about."

"I worry about you being sad about the pearly harbor, Pop," said Lily.

"When do we eat?" asked Pete.

There wasn't much Pearl Harbor news really, just ordinary Sunday shows—the New York Philharmonic and other music, *One Man's Family,* Jack Benny, Edgar Bergen and Charlie McCarthy—interrupted now and again with updates about bombs and fires and sunken ships. *"It's no joke,"* one announcer said. *"It's a real war."* But it seemed unreal, as if the war didn't bother Jack Benny and Rochester, and people were laughing and not at all afraid.

Neighbors dropped in and out, bringing rumors of paratroopers and dive-bombers in Honolulu and Japanese warships heading toward the California coast. Pop changed radio stations frequently, but what little news they had was contradictory. It was obvious no one knew what the truth was. The more worried the grown-ups got, the more afraid I was. My stomach clenched like a fist, and my right eyelid twitched. Lily climbed back onto the sofa with Pete and me, and I held the two of them close.

It was dark before we thought to eat. The light from giant searchlights swept the sky, casting strange shadows through our windows. Our burgers were cold and greasy but I didn't care. I wasn't hungry anyway. *It's no joke, it's a real war* played over and over in my head.

"Will the Japanese invade us?" I asked.

"Will bombs kill us?" Lily wanted to know.

And Pete, a worried frown on his sticky face, asked, "Will we still have Christmas?"

No one knew the answers. Lily and Pete fell asleep on the sofa, and the radio played on.

Sherlock Holmes was interrupted by an announcement that all lights were to be turned off so as not to aid enemy aircraft. And then the radio stations went off the air. My face and hands grew cold, and I tensed up, waiting in the silent darkness.

After a while in the dark, Pop stood up. He and Mama hugged us extra tight. Even Edna got a hug. And the McGonigle family went to bed.

Sometime later I was awakened by the noise of airplanes flying overhead, maybe ours from the naval air station on North Island, maybe the Japanese or Germans. I sat up and wrapped my arms around my knees, waiting for incoming bombs or paratroopers with machine guns or who knows what. War scenes from movies and newsreels flashed across my mind. I felt sick.

"We're scared," Lily said, wheezing, as she and Pete climbed into the big bed.

"Can we sleep with you?" they asked together. Edna grumbled and moved to the sofa.

I was haunted by my own fears and worries. My body felt jangled, like I had electricity instead of blood in my veins. But I was, after all, the big sister and felt an unexpected stab of responsibility. "Okay, but you, Petey, have to promise not to wet the bed. And, Lily, no hogging the covers." They snuggled in and Lily stuck her thumb in her mouth.

"Are those planes from bad guys?" Pete asked. "Are they going to bomb us?"

"Will we have war here?" Lily asked, her face all wrinkled with worry.

And from Pete: "Just what is war?"

Bombs and guns and fear and death and suffering, I thought, but said, "Don't you guys worry about war. Remember when we used to get the comics in the Sunday paper? Remember Superman? He flies around fighting criminals and spies, remember? That's who we hear up there. Not the Japanese. Superman. *Whoosh. Swoop.* There he is again. Chasing away the bad guys. Keeping us safe. Thanks, Superman."

"And Supergirl," said Lily.

Pete snorted. "There's no Supergirl."

"Why not?" I asked. "She could be up there fighting Nazis and Japan and spies just like Superman. And Buck Rogers and Flash Gordon will come from the future to help. The bad guys are doomed."

"If I could fly, I'd pound them," Pete said as he snuggled closer and closed his eyes.

"Tell us a story," Lily said, "about Lily and Pete fighting the bad guys."

So I did. I told them about Pete commanding a submarine that wiped out the Japanese navy, and Lily piloting an airplane, bombing the Nazis. I thought Lily the pill could likely annoy the Germans into submission, but the very idea of Pete in a war terrified me. Soon they fell asleep, comforted. I felt shivers of fright at the sound of planes overhead, but finally, lulled by the warmth and the rhythm of Pete's soft snoring, I, too, relaxed a little. But what would tomorrow bring?

DECEMBER 14, 1941
SUNDAY

It had been the worst week of my whole life. Well, second worst to when Gram died. I asked a few neighbors if they knew anyone who had died in the bombing at Pearl Harbor, but they all looked at me funny and said, "No, thank goodness." That wasn't helpful for my book, so I just wrote **MCGONIGLE** in the sand over and over, though I feared nothing could keep us safe now.

I was afraid to be away from Mama and Pop on that Monday in case something else bad happened, so they let Lily and me stay home from school. We heard President Roosevelt declare war on Japan, as if Japan hadn't already done so with their bombs. *December 7, 1941. A date which will live in infamy,* the president called it. Then Germany and Italy declared war on the United States. It was war, real war.

What little news we heard was all bad. The Pacific Fleet had been wiped out. Dead and wounded ran into the thousands. The Japanese invaded the Philippines and Guam and other South Seas islands like those Dorothy Lamour made movies about.

I jumped at every unexpected noise, and my fingernails were nearly chewed off. Sirens wailed day and night. No one knew whether they were false alarms or drills or the real thing. The radio spread rumors of Japanese planes, and ships, and submarines preparing to attack the West Coast. Planes with the Japanese emblem of a rising sun on their wings were spotted over San Francisco. Unidentified planes were reported flying toward San Diego, and the city was blacked out, perfectly dark from sundown to sunup every day, no lights anywhere, to avoid letting enemy aircraft know we were here. Mama declared that we would sleep in our clothes and have suitcases packed and ready in case we had to evacuate in a hurry. The rumors turned out to be false alarms, but my suitcase stayed packed.

We were now involved in three wars, with Germany, Italy, and Japan. How could we fight nearly the whole rest of the world? Well, not England, I knew, but plenty of the world. I wished for the millionth time Gram were here to talk to.

But Gram was not around, so I went to look for Rosie. She was sitting outside the Fribbles', doing homework. "It's war, Rosie. Isn't it awful?"

"Not as awful as living with the Fribbles or"—she waved her paper around—"working with square roots. I think square roots are the most useless mathematical function in the world." More waving of paper ensued. "What's their use? I mean, do you go into a store and say, 'I'd like to buy the square root of sixty seven cents' worth of candy, please'?" She crumpled up her paper and threw it over her shoulder. "Square roots are so unhip, which is why they're called square." She chuckled at her own joke.

"Be serious, Rosie. We're at war. A real war. What do you think will happen to us? Will we be invaded? Bombed? I'm scared."

"War is awful, and I hope it stays far away from here. But don't get all panicky until we know what it means. One day at a time. One day at a time." And she bent over her homework again.

"Holy mackerel, you're so cool and unconcerned. Don't you care?" It seemed a little creepy to me.

Rosie looked up from her papers and lifted one eyebrow. "Loosen up, Millie."

Loosen up? Easy for her to say. Last Wednesday morning I'd awakened to rain, flashes of light, and great thundering booms. Fear stuck in my throat. "Bombs!" Pete cried from the sofa, which started Lily crying and Edna muttering *"Mein Gott! Mein Gott!"* over and over.

"Quiet! Quiet!" Pop shouted from our doorway. "Must be a thunderstorm in the mountains. Not a bomb. Just a thunderstorm."

"Are you sure?" Lily asked, and Pop nodded.

In the silence that followed, Pete called out, "So what? I wasn't scared."

"Me neither," said Lily, but she climbed into the big bed and snuggled next to me, dragging the doll she now called Supergirl.

Me, I'd been plenty scared. I'd been scared for so long, and I was still scared. Was the worst here? Or would there be worse to come? I shuddered. "Toodle-oo, Rosie," I said. "I'm outta here." And I went home.

"What do you think of your Hitler now?" Pop asked Edna at dinner.

"*My* Hitler? Nonsense. I never cared for the man. He's no good. You can tell from his face. All sour and frowny." Edna lifted her fork like a sword. "From now on, nothing German will pass my lips. No sauerkraut, no hamburgers, no frankfurters, no beer. They're all *verboten*—I mean, forbidden!"

"What's wrong with frankfurters?" I asked.

"Named for Frankfurt, Germany. Forbidden!"

"And hamburgers?"

"Hamburg, Germany, of course. Very creative in the kitchen, those Germans," Edna said.

Lily whined. "Will Pop be in trouble? He makes hamburgers at the Burger Shack."

"Pop makes American hamburgers," Pete said.

Edna frowned. "Doesn't matter. Hamburgers are hamburgers. German."

"Be careful, Edna. Watch out for German measles," said Pop.

"And German shepherds," I said.

"And ger-aniums," Pete added.

"Go ahead, make fun, but I'm serious. Since Italy declared war, I am thinking of banning spaghetti also. Now, who has seen my glasses?"

They were on her head and we all laughed. It felt good. Not much is funny during a war.

"Are you seeing Albert today?" Mama asked Edna.

"No. Albert is history—he's too serious, too funny-looking, and he smells like mothballs. I'm going to the movies with Ruby Heller."

"I'm sorry," said Mama. "Albert was a real gentleman and I think he genuinely liked you."

"Who cares? The war will bring plenty of sailors to San Diego." And Edna left.

"With the war, will we still have Christmas?" Pete asked once again.

"I want to talk to you kids about that," Pop said. "Because of our money troubles and the war, Christmas will be a little skimpy this year."

"War, war, war! I'm sick of hearing about the war!" Lily whined. "Now it will ruin Christmas!"

"Enough, or we won't have any Christmas at all!" shouted Pop. There was silence. "What money we have will go for blackout curtains, batteries, flashlights, candles, and matches we'll need. So your mother and I decided that we'll make presents for each other instead of buying them. Mr. Sears has enough money already."

I groaned.

"What about Santa?" asked Pete. "Will he still bring us presents this year? I think we've been good. Or good enough."

Pop winked at me. "Oh, I think Santa will have a few presents for you, Petey, but it may be socks and underwear," he said.

"*Nerts!*" said Pete.

"Language, Pete," said Mama, coming in with a cardboard carton.

"What's wrong with *nerts*? It just means *nuts!*"

"Then say *nuts*. On second thought, don't say *nuts*. Just nod politely and agree." She set the box down on the table.

"This is full of things left over from our old store—fabric pieces, needles and thread, buttons, yarn, ribbons and string, feathers, sequins, paper clips, rubber bands, all sorts of stuff."

"You have crayons and scissors and paste," Pop said. "See what you guys can come up with."

Holy moly. I'd been hoping for new oarlocks for the boat. Now I'd likely get sequined bookmarks, a paper-clip necklace, and a button bracelet. I guessed that was only fair since that was what I'd be giving, but still . . . I cut and sewed and pasted and muttered about how unfair life was.

After dinner Mama and I hung heavy blankets over all the windows in the house, which we'd use until we could buy official blackout curtains. I went outside to make sure not even a pinprick of light showed. The house was totally dark, as was the rest of San Diego. Occasional searchlights pierced the sky, but streetlights and neon signs were unlit. It was eerie. I missed seeing lit windows up and down the beach and headlights crossing the causeway. How would drivers find their way in the darkness with their lights off?

There had been a bonfire up the beach. Probably the Graysons roasting marshmallows. As I watched, the fire flickered and ebbed and died, and there was not a glimmer of light left on earth. I shivered—it felt like I was on another planet. But there was no blackout for the moon, and a million stars shone in the dark sky.

DECEMBER 22, 1941
MONDAY

I sat on the beach, skipping stones on the water and contemplating my new life. No Japanese planes had attacked Mission Beach, but San Diego was changing fast. Planes roared overhead day and night, soldiers and sailors crowded the downtown streets, buses overflowed with defense-factory workers in overalls. Sometimes men who were not in uniform were taunted and called draft dodgers, even if it wasn't their fault. Like Pop.

Pop's heart murmur kept him out of the army. He got a job as a clerk at the Navy Exchange, so it was almost like he got his store back. Mama bought eye protectors and started welding school at night.

School was out for Christmas break until 1942, and I was delighted to be away for a while. It was a nightmare. The windows were covered with heavy black curtains, and air-raid-drill sirens screamed every day. Instead of arithmetic and history, we spent our days practicing for air raids by huddling in hallways and hiding under desks. Kids played war games instead of kickball and hopscotch and looked for someone to pick on.

The *Give to Polish War Relief* posters taped up in Mr. Bell's store windows and the post office had been replaced with *Uncle Sam Wants You for the U.S. Army!* and *Enlist! Our Men Out There Need Your Help.* One poster showed sweaty bare-chested sailors in a submarine loading torpedoes over the words *Man the Guns! Join the Navy!*

All the soldiers and sailors on recruiting posters were muscular, and tough, and very handsome, unlike the young, spindly, scared-looking fellows I saw taking the bus to the Navy Recruiting Station. How many of them would end up in my Book of Dead Things? Could I tell by looking in their faces who would die and who would live?

I scoured the beach looking for something, anything, to add to my book. Something to keep us alive and safe. There were plenty of sand crabs but I wanted to add something impressive, like a giant squid or a blue whale. No luck, so I turned for home.

Pete and MeToo and Ralphie Rigoletto had traded in their ray guns for driftwood rifles, and they were marching in front of our house, shouting, *"Hup! Hup! Hup!"* Icky pulled up and began pelting Ralphie with stones. "Go home, spaghetti eater," he shouted at Ralphie. "You Italians are as bad as the Germans. Go back to Italy with your hero Mussolini!"

"I'm not Italian," Ralphie insisted. "I'm one hundred percent American. I hate spaghetti, and I don't even know any *muscle-beanie*!"

"Knock it off, Icky," I said.

"Who's that telling me what to do?" Icky said, throwing a stone in my direction.

"I am, for one," said Pop as he came down the walk. Icky the coward ran off, and Pop took Ralphie's arm. "You're not the enemy, Ralphie. Be proud of being American and Italian."

"I love spaghetti," Pete said, patting Ralphie's back.

Ralphie grinned. "So do I, really."

Pop and I went into the house, followed by Pete, Ralphie, and MeToo, *blam-blam*ing and *pow-pow*ing their make-believe rifles. Lily was trying to get her doll, which she was currently calling Mrs. Santa, to hold a crayon. And Mama had just come home from a Red Cross meeting with yarn and knitting needles. "Thousands of women across the country are knitting for servicemen," she said, "making socks, sweaters, mufflers, blankets, even knitted bandages. In San Diego there's a group of Japanese American women, brokenhearted over Pearl Harbor, who are knitting, too. We're all knitting to help the U.S. win the war."

"Do you know how to knit?" I asked her. "I never saw you."

"We got quick instruction this morning. It didn't look too hard." Pointing to a big bag of army green yarn, she said, "Lots of young people are knitting—nothing fancy. Squares to link together for blankets for soldiers. That's what we'll do, Millie."

"Do I have to?" I thought it might be sort of interesting, but I wasn't about to say that.

"Let me! Let me!" Pete yelled, dropping his wooden rifle and bounding over.

"Me too," said MeToo, a toothless grin on his dirty, freckled face.

"I have three sets of needles," Mama said. "One for Millie and one for me, and I thought Lily might like to join us."

"Uh-uh," said Lily. "Mrs. Santa and I are drawing pictures to send to soldiers."

Mama gave knitting needles to Pete and me and showed us how to get the yarn on the needles and a knitting stitch. Pete tangled the yarn before he even got it near the needles. "Crumb!" he shouted. "Girls do the dumbest things." He grabbed his rifle and ran out the door, Ralphie following.

"Let me try," said MeToo, pressed against my side, watching closely.

Sure, I thought. *You won't last even as long as Pete.* "Okay." I handed him Pete's discarded needles. "Go ahead and see if you can do it."

He could, and faster than me. And Mama. So the three of us settled on the sofa, knitting army green squares for blankets for soldiers.

Soon enough Pete came back inside. "Come play with us, Lily. We need you."

Lily shook her head. "No way. You make girls be Nazis."

"We gotta have enemies or it's no fun."

She shook her head again and went back to coloring.

I finally finished a square—well, an almost-square with only a few dropped stitches. It looked pretty good to me, and better than Mama's, which was kind of like a washcloth with buttonholes. "Here's my square. I'm finished."

"Me too," said MeToo, and he handed his neat, perfect, buttonhole-free squares to Mama. Five of them to my one.

I'll be a monkey's uncle, I thought. MeToo was a natural.

Mama and I packed in our needles and left MeToo sitting happily, turning out square after square. I walked up Bayside Walk hoping to find Rosie. I hadn't talked with her since our "one day at a time" conversation. Did she still feel as unconcerned about the war? Were we still friends?

There she was, sitting on a towel on the sand, wearing a white bathing suit like Rita Hayworth, her nose gleaming white from a coat of zinc oxide. Her hair—her wavy red hair, not stringy and bleached from the sun like mine—bounced on her shoulders. She smiled at me. We were okay.

I flopped down next to her.

"What's buzzin', cousin?" she asked. Rosie was much more hip and sophisticated than I was. I guessed she was asking *What's up?*

"Not much. Just hanging around," I told her.

"Me too. Don't you love vacations?" she asked. "I was sick of school. Since the war started, it's like a zoo there. Guys squabble about who will enlist first and who's too chicken and what they'd do to the enemy but wind up shoving and fighting each other instead. And the girls stand around and giggle."

"You're telling *me* about zoos. Icky and his buddies act like idiots, marching around with black combs held under their noses, pretending to be Hitler."

Rosie shook her head. "That makes quite a picture. I'd like to laugh but it's not funny."

"No, it's mean. Even grown-ups are doing dumb things. Danny Fellers says his dad sits in his car with a loaded shotgun every night looking for anything suspicious. I think some poor alley cat will get his tail shot off." I turned over on my back, chewing on my lip in thought. "Sometimes I pretend the U.S. is at war with Ireland and I'm considered *the enemy* to see what that would feel like. But I know it's only make-believe. I can be sorry for Japanese and German and Italian kids, but I can't really feel what they feel even when I try."

"Guess you're just lucky Ireland hasn't dropped any bombs on us."

"Do you still not worry about the war coming here? Aren't you afraid?"

Rosie rubbed suntan lotion on her legs. "I can't do anything about it. I'll just wait and see what happens."

"But what happens could be awful."

Rosie shrugged. "I'm just not a worrier."

"What about your mother? Are you at least worried about her? That she might . . . well, you know, die?"

"She's been sick most of my life. I'm pretty used to it." Rosie lay down on her towel. "But sometimes I get angry with her even though it isn't her fault she's sick. Doesn't seem fair, does it? But I can't help it."

I remembered Pete and his anger about the Lone Ranger dying. And now Rosie. Was it possible to love someone and be angry with them at the same time? I frowned and changed the subject. "You're fourteen, aren't you?"

"Yeah. Why?"

"Well, I'm tired of reading cheery kiddie books from the library. I need to learn more about death and suffering and war, but I'm not thirteen yet, so I'm confined to the baby section. If you'd check out some adult books for me, I'd be ever so grateful."

"Sounds awfully grim, Mil, but I guess I could do it as long as I don't have to read them, too. What books do you want?"

I chewed my lip. "I'll have to think and make a list."

A shriek like a siren rang out from the Fribbles' house. "Rosemary Fribble, get in here now. Your mama needs you." Rosie frowned, waved, and went.

At dinner, Edna announced that she was applying to be an air-raid warden.

"What's an airy dwarden?" Lily asked.

"They tell people what to do if bombs come. And make sure no light is shining during blackouts. They're important. People have to pay attention to them. And they wear armbands, helmets, and whistles." Edna smiled. "I'd like to be important."

Mama and Pop looked at each other. "Edna, is that wise?" Mama asked. "You have been . . . you know . . . you aren't . . ."

"I know, I know. I forget things, lose things, do stupid things. I think I have a screw loose in my head. But I'm tired of being useless. I'm sure I can do this. The Civilian Defense volunteer-training people will teach me. And I really want that whistle."

Pete whooped. "I want a whistle, too. And a helmet. I know what to do if bombs come."

"You don't," Lily said.

"Do so. Shoot back and then hide."

I laughed. Pete had all the answers.

DECEMBER 28, 1941
SUNDAY

A Santa Ana wind screamed all night, blowing sand against the windows and rattling doors, making everyone tense and irritable, so when Lily came into the big bed early in the morning, making it much too crowded, and started snuffling about her stiff neck, I was having none of it. "Can it, Lily. Don't be such a baby," I said, and turned over to go back to sleep. Lily crept back to her own bed, moaning and whimpering.

"Mama! Lily's making so much noise that Cousin Edna and I can't sleep." In truth Cousin Edna was sawing logs on her side of the bed, making much more noise than Lily. "Come and make Lily be quiet!"

Mama cooed softly to Lily before turning to me. "Lily is awfully hot. Get some cool cloths for her head."

I grumbled my way into the bathroom and wet a wash-cloth for Lily. Still, her fever stayed high all morning, and she moaned louder and louder, grabbing for her neck and twitching her legs. Her Shirley Temple curls clung limp and wet to her head.

Since Garland's polio, Mama had been inspecting us daily for headaches, muscle pains, and fever, and now I could see the panic in her face. Was Lily getting sicker? Was it polio? Could Pete catch it? Or me? My heart thumped.

On his way to work, Pop dropped Pete at Ralphie's house to keep him out of germs' way. I stayed at home in case Mama needed me, still in my pajamas, looking at the Sears catalog. I hadn't decided what to do with my jingle prize money. Oarlocks? A new book? Or something fun like a harmonica or a music box that plays "When Irish Eyes Are Smiling"? Worrying about what to choose kept me from chewing at my nails and thinking about getting polio.

At noon, Mama, her voice low and tight, said, "Millie, go to Bell's and ask to use the telephone. I know it's Sunday and they won't be open but Mr. Bell will let you use it. Call Dr. Peterson and ask him to come see Lily right away."

I jumped into slacks and a sweater and ran. What if it was polio? I imagined Lily in a big metal tube with only her head sticking out. Do people with polio die? What if Lily died? Would I have to add her to my Book of Dead Things? I shuddered. Sure, Lily was a pill, but I didn't want her to die. And did I have to call her that so often? She couldn't help it that she was pale and sickly and took so much of Mama's attention.

Mr. Bell was happy to let me use the telephone. Dr. Peterson was out of town, but a Dr. Conway was covering and would be along when he could. While we waited, Mama and I worked together cooling Lily down when she burned and warming her up when she shivered. It wasn't much but it felt good to be doing something.

Lily's complaints came in croaks. Her throat was sore, her neck stiff. "Lily, if you just get well," I told her, "I'll be much nicer to you and I won't call you a pill anymore."

Finally Lily fell into a restless sleep. Mama put her arm around my shoulders.

"I'm sorry that Lily is so sick," I said to her. "I know she is your favorite and—"

"My favorite? Why would you say that?"

"It's always Lily first in everything. Lily gets a bed to herself. She never has to run to the store or empty the garbage or help make dinner. And when you call us, it's *Lily and Millie and Pete.* When you talk about us, it's the same—*Lily and Millie and Pete.* Lily is always first."

Mama's face crumpled. "I guess you're right," she said softly. "I always think of you three that way: *Lily and Millie and Pete.* I see you, Millie, standing there, their hands in yours, protecting them, being there for them to lean on and hang on to." She squeezed me hard. "Millie, in the middle, the rock, keeping them safe. I count on you, Millie, my beloved oldest girl."

My throat tightened. Was I getting sick, too? But I was merely holding tears in. Beloved? Me?

"I once saw a picture of a medieval cathedral in England," Mama went on, "two slender towers, one at each side of a tall central section that looked solid and strong. It reminded me of you children, Lily and Pete flanking my tall, sturdy Millie. I wrote a poem about it."

Like a medieval cathedral,
Two spires leaning against the center,

The anchor, the mainstay, the linchpin.
Safe because they stand together,
Strong because they stand together.
My Lily and Millie and Pete.

That did it. Tears pushed their way past the lump in my throat. I gulped and sniffled, hugged Mama, and hurried outside before my blubbers woke Lily. Was I beloved? Did Mama really count on me? Why didn't she tell me more often?

What with blackouts, siren tests, rumors, and bookmarks and pincushions for presents, it had been a weird Christmas, but the bay seemed untroubled. A crowd of sandpipers, in San Diego for a winter vacation, tottered on their long, spindly legs in search of insects for dinner. An oystercatcher pranced past with a sand crab in its red beak. They didn't know or care about the war, about Lily's sickness, about polio and money troubles and Jungle Gardenia. Sometimes I wished I were a bird.

When I finally returned to the house, the doctor had come. I waited outside, worrying. Was it polio? If so, was it my fault for not keeping the Book of Dead Things better? Did I not write enough **MCGONIGLE**s in the sand? I was getting a little bored with it all, but would I disappoint Gram and put us at risk if I stopped? What would life be like without Lily, Lily with the blond curls and silly doll? I thought I'd like to be sisterless, but it turned out I was wrong. And I was scared.

When I finally went inside, the doctor was leaving. No, it wasn't polio, he said, but a very bad flu, a serious issue because of Lily's lung troubles. "Keep her in bed and quiet," he said. "Push liquids to keep her hydrated."

Mama hugged me in joy and relief. Not polio! I felt a sort of release. The day seemed a bit brighter. Even the wind had stopped. The doctor repacked his bag and walked toward the door. "I charge five dollars for a house call on a Sunday, and I prefer to be paid on the spot straightaway."

Five dollars! Mama paled. "Dr. Peterson always left a bill and we paid when we could."

"I prefer not to bill but to be paid, as I said, on the spot." Dr. Conway stuck out his hand.

Mama fumbled in her purse. "I don't have enough at the moment, but . . ."

The doctor frowned, and Mama's face turned red.

There was no other way. I sighed and got my five-dollar bill—my precious jingle-prize five-dollar bill, my harmonica and music-box and oarlock money—and gave it to Mama to pay the doctor. She squeezed my hand, and I felt a little less resentful. And a bit proud.

The new year can't come soon enough, I thought as I tumbled into bed that night. 1941 had ended badly. But Lily would be okay, and I'd hold on to that.

JANUARY 3, 1942
SATURDAY

I buttoned my jacket as I left the house. It was winter in San Diego, which meant sixty-two degrees, and a cool morning breeze blew in from the sea. A group of octopus fishermen were on the beach, shouting and digging and laughing, and I waved as I kicked through the mud looking for dead things. The mud provided bits of broken clamshells, a bird foot, and a hermit crab hiding in a snail shell, and I sketched them in my book. I tossed the shells and the crab back into the water, where they belonged. The bird foot I buried in the sand. I tucked the book back into my jacket pocket and gave it a few pats.

The radio said the Japanese had invaded Manila in the Philippines. I didn't know where that was but it sounded too close for me. I scrolled a **MCGONIGLE** in the mud and then, just to be sure, wrote it again. **MCGONIGLE.**

On Bayside Walk I saw Edna, off to her first Civilian Defense volunteer training wearing a hat with a gold feather perched on her black hair and, in honor of the special occasion, extra Jungle Gardenia. "I hope I get my whistle today," she said as she teetered on her high heels up the walk.

It was nearly noon when I returned, and the house was quiet. Lily was still in bed, surrounded by books, crayons, and a plate of toast crusts. Pop was at the Navy Exchange, Pete was at Ralphie's, and Mama, who was now working a twelve-hour night shift at Consolidated Aircraft, was just waking up and coming into the kitchen. Lily jumped up and threw her arms around Mama's waist. "I miss you, Mama," she said.

"And I miss you, chickadee."

"Stay home, Mama. Don't go." Lily held up her doll. "You can play with her if you stay."

"It's a war, Lily-billy. We all make sacrifices. Mine is missing my babies."

And mine, I thought, *is having to take care of these little nuisances when both Mama and Pop are gone.* But I didn't say it out loud, and that was an even greater sacrifice.

"What's for dinner?" Pete asked Mama, munching on half a cheese sandwich as he entered the kitchen.

"Dinner? You're still eating lunch."

"I need to make plans."

"You'll have to ask your father," Mama said. "He's the cook now. For the duration of the war, I'll be making airplanes, not dinner."

"Pop's cooking? Then I'm going back to Ralphie's. They're having beef stew."

"Have you been invited?"

"I will be. I just need to look cute and hungry."

And he was gone again.

"Sometimes I think he's my phantom son, not really here, just a whiff and a memory." Mama finished her coffee with a sigh.

Lily and I were doing homework at the table when Mama left. "I need help, Millie," Lily said. "I don't know how to do this."

"This what?"

"This! Add 37 and 85. I know 7 and 5 are 12, so I write down 12. And 8 and 3 are 11, so I write down 11. Then what do I do? Add 12 and 11? Or should I add 3 and 7 and 8 and 5?"

"Neither. Start again. Remember what you've learned about the *ones* place and the *tens* place?"

"Sort of. Well, no."

"Well, 7 and 5 are in the ones place and they add up to 12, which is 10 and 2, so the 2 goes in the ones place but the 1 goes in the tens place, so—"

"Millie, I can't understand that. Just tell me the right answer." She dropped her head to the table.

Lily's flu had left her a bit weak and much less annoying. Or maybe the thought of being without her had left me more tolerant. I reached over and fluffed her hair. "Nope. We'll work on it together until you get it." And we did.

The house was quiet again until Pete blew in with slamming doors and thudding feet. "Where's the shovel?" he asked me.

"Likely outside where you last left it."

Pete left for a few minutes but soon returned with more

door slamming. "I have a message for you from Dicky Fribble." Pete stuck his thumbs in his ears and waggled his fingers. "Is there any message I should take back?"

"Yes. *Drop dead*. Tell him to drop dead."

Pete nodded and took a pancake turner and serving spoons from a drawer. I grabbed his sleeve as he passed. "Where are you taking those?"

"It's a surprise."

"Better bring them back just like you found them."

I'd just finished my homework when Pop came home and started supper. His specialties were Chef Boy-Ar-Dee canned spaghetti and Kraft boxed macaroni and cheese. One dyed our lips red and the other bright orange.

"Where's Pete?" Pop asked, waving a spoon like a bandleader.

"He's having dinner at Ralphie's."

Actually at the moment Pete was outside calling me. He was pulling Ralphie's wagon with something under a towel. It wasn't Pepperoni the turtle, who had died and was now just a page in my book. This was something lumpish and stinky. I wrinkled my nose. "What you got there, bud? Buried treasure?"

"Exactly. Come see. It's for you."

I went closer. The smell got worse. Not fishy but bad. Real bad. What was it?

"Ta-da!" whooped Pete, and he whipped the towel off the lump in the wagon.

I pinched my nose closed and went closer still. It was an animal. Maybe a cat. No, a dog. Or mostly skeleton with clumps of dog still attached.

"Yikes, Pete! How grotesque."

"Icky Fribble and I dug it up on the beach. He said it's a present for you. I thought you'd like it for your Book of Dead Things. I call it Pluto, like Mickey Mouse's dog." Pete's face was eager and hopeful. "Do you like it? I'm pretty sure it's dead."

Pop came out. "What on earth is that smell?"

"It's a dog," said Pete. "It's Millie's."

"Millie's? Well, Millie, take it and bury it somewhere far away."

"But it's—"

"Just do it. Why in blazes would you bring it here? You should know better."

"But I didn't—"

"Go! And don't touch it. Pete, you come inside and wash your hands. I'll start the macaroni and cheese."

I tucked my book and a pencil in my pocket so I could draw the dog before I disposed of it. It certainly was a dead thing. Off I went, pulling the wagon that reeked of dead dog. Christopher Columbus! Luckily there were not too many people around to see me. Or smell me.

It was so unfair. Icky Fribble dumped a dead dog on me, Pete lugged it home, and I'm punished for it. Pete gets two dinners, and one was beef stew. And the mac and cheese would likely be gone before I got even one bright orange mouthful.

I dragged the wagon and its cargo on Bayside Walk toward the south end of the beach. If I buried the dog back in its hole, some other little kid might find it. Besides, I was tired and hungry and had no shovel for digging. Pete must have left it somewhere. I looked out at the water. Yes, of course! This dog deserved to be buried at sea. That's what they do for dead heroes in seafaring movies. And all dogs are heroes.

I didn't want to drop it into the bay. Low tide could very well expose it again. It had to be the ocean. The west side of the bridge, which connected the south end of Mission Beach to the town of Ocean Beach, faced the open ocean. There were never very many people there this time of day, so I could launch the skeleton over the side into the water without attracting too much attention.

The wheels on the wagon squeaked and clattered on the walk as I pulled it toward the bridge. Poor Pluto. How did he die? Was he sick? Did he suffer? Would his bones sink slowly into the water or be swept out to sea? To Hawaii, maybe, where the water would be warm and gentle? I hoped so.

I maneuvered the wagon as close as I could get it to the edge of the bridge and unwrapped the skeleton. The sky was clouding and the wind rising, and the smell was getting worse. I decided not to stay and draw the dog in my book but just list his name: *Pluto Dog, died San Diego, 1942.* Holding my breath, I wrapped the skeleton in the towel and, ugh, picked it up. It wasn't too heavy, being mostly bones. As I lifted it, the skull poked out, and the lower jawbone, teeth bared, fell to the ground. It was foul, grim, revolting . . . but definitely intriguing. That I'd keep to draw carefully in my book.

I dropped the dog into the sea but kept hold of the towel. I'd have liked to throw the reeking, rattling wagon in, too, but Ralphie would want it back, even stinking of dog, of death.

The dog's bones bobbed on the surface for a minute and then slowly sank from sight. "Farewell, Pluto," I murmured. "I'm sure you were a good dog and someone cared enough to bury you when you died, but you're a putrid old thing now. Goodbye and sleep well." It was silly to be mourning for a dog, especially a dog skeleton, but I was all at once bursting with misery. My eyes and my nose ran, and I bit my lip to stop them as I wiped my face with my hand.

Once home, I sat in front of our cottage and drew the jawbone in my book. *Thanks, Pluto, for leaving me your jaw,* I thought. Pluto was gone but he had left something of himself behind. Like people do. Not jawbones but memories and silver hairbrushes. I felt a quick twinge of, maybe, gratitude.

The jawbone was brownish white, with several yellow teeth, one broken. Had the dog been in a fight or hit by a car? I was growing mournful again. What should I do with the bone? I could throw it in the water, too, or bury it . . . but I thought of something better. Yes! I would share the stinky dog fangs with someone who deserved them.

I tore a page out of my book and wrote *To Icky from Pluto. Did you miss me? Don't have nightmares now!* and tucked the note in with the bone and wrapped them in the towel. The jawbone and I hurried to the Fribbles' and rang the doorbell. I ran away but Pluto's jaw stayed right there on Icky's doorstep.

JANUARY 4, 1942
SUNDAY

Pete pulled at my blanket. "Millie, I'm not sleepy. And I'm hungry."

"Go away. It's the middle of the night." It wasn't really, but the sun hadn't risen yet. "Do you want to climb in here?"

"No. I'm awake, and I'm hungry." He pulled again, harder.

"Okay, okay. Be quiet and don't wake anybody else. I'll come sit with you, and if it's not foggy, we can watch the stars go out."

I made us a cheese sandwich to share and pulled a chair up to the living room window. Pete curled in my lap. I could smell his sweet and sweaty little-boy smell.

"What stars am I seeing?" he asked.

I'm no astronomer but I have a pretty good imagination. "See there—that bunch of stars followed by a long tail? That's the constellation Squirrel. And those stars sprinkled around are Sky Oysters and Clams and Heavenly Corn Flakes."

"How do you know so much?"

"I'm pretty old. I've been around."

Pete giggled and I squeezed him.

"Where do stars go when they go out?" he asked.

"Oh, they're still there. They just pull their blankets up to their chins and go to sleep."

"Look, Millie. There are new stars coming out on the bridge over there."

"Those are the lights of cars crossing the causeway to downtown. It must be almost morning. The blackout is over. We'll see the sun rise soon."

"One, two, three . . . four!" Pete sat happily counting cars until we heard Pop.

"Anybody for CheeriOats?" Pop asked.

"Me! Me!" said Pete, jumping down from my lap, which felt suddenly cold and sort of lonely.

"But you already ate," I told him.

"I'm hungry again. Counting stars is hard work." He took the box of cereal and poured until his bowl was over-flowing. "Look," he said. "Baby doughnuts!"

After breakfast, Dwayne Fribble came by with Pluto's towel-wrapped jawbone. He said Mrs. Fribble was hysterical with fear and disgust. Why did they assume it was me who left it? Pop said I had to take the bone and give it a proper burial. But first, I had to write a letter of apology to the Fribbles.

My first try—*Sorry, but it's actually Icky's fault because he dug up the dog and didn't dispose of it properly but sent it to me, the crumb*—Pop called snarkish and insincere. "Try again," he said.

Second try—*I'm sorry I scared and disgusted Mrs. Fribble. I apologize to her, Dicky, and the dog*—was deemed a poor effort, but since I wrote *Dicky* instead of *Icky* this time, Pop said it would likely do.

On the way to the Fribbles' house, I buried the jawbone in an out-of-the-way patch of sand and saluted. *Farewell again, Pluto.* I took the letter and slipped it under the Fribbles' door. I couldn't face any Fribbles this early in the morning.

When I got back, I took Lily and Pete outside so Mama could sleep. I automatically took my Book of Dead Things with me.

"Why do you take that book everywhere?" Lily asked. "Is it important?"

Did I? Was it? "No, of course not. That would be dumb. And weird. It's just a notebook."

"Then why do you always take it?"

"I don't. See, I'm leaving it right here on the table."

But before I'd gotten out the door, I turned back for the book. I just didn't feel right leaving it behind.

"Let's build a sand castle," said Lily, tiptoeing through the mud on the beach.

"There's no sand here," Pete said. "We can build a mud fort, in case we're invaded by Japanese submarines!"

Lily squealed and pointed. "Eek, I think I see one!"

"Don't be silly, Lily. There are no submarines in the bay. It's way too shallow."

But we built a fort anyway, with driftwood gun turrets and a paper-bag flag. And then we had an eelgrass fight. And skipped stones. And let Mama sleep.

Hundreds of moon jellies lay stranded on the beach, as

they were every winter and spring after a high tide. I lifted one up. "Look, guys, you can see your hand right through them."

"Can I pick one up?" Pete asked.

"Sure, but don't step on them. You'd be like Charlie Chaplin and a banana peel. And be sure and wash your hands after so you don't irritate your eyes."

I pulled my book from a pocket and, studying the jellies closely, started to draw. Each was the size of a large pancake and so translucent I could see a stomach or something right through them. From what I could tell, they didn't have a brain, heart, blood, head, eyes, or ears. Life couldn't be much fun for moon jellies.

Lily saw me with the notebook and gave me a questioning look. Who cared what she thought? I kept drawing dead moon jellies in my unimportant book.

Edna was in the bathroom when we returned. "Why aren't you at air-raid-warden training?" I asked her.

"Phooey. Too much work. They wanted me to learn rules and maps and streets. My memory's not that good. So I quit." She lifted her foot onto the toilet seat and began to draw a line up the back of her leg with her eyebrow pencil.

"What on earth are you doing?"

She changed legs. "Because of the war, there's no silk or nylon for stockings. It seems the army needs it for parachutes. I make fake seams up my legs so it looks like I'm wearing stockings." She examined each leg. "Fortunately I have a little tan, so I don't need leg makeup like some other gals do."

Yes, Edna had some tan, but also lots of blue veins, a bruise or two, and crooked seams, but on the whole it was not too bad.

She wrapped a scarf like a turban around her hair and added more lipstick to her red mouth. "Albert is taking me downtown to lunch at the U.S. Grant Hotel. It's very expensive." Edna pressed her lips together to set the lipstick. "He really likes me."

"I thought Albert was history."

"We'll see," said Edna with a small smile.

Mama was up and about when Albert arrived. In he came, as spindly and bigheaded as I remembered.

Lily and Pete hadn't met him before. Lily squeaked and hid behind Mama's skirts. Pete inhaled sharply, and I feared what was coming next. "How does your giant head balance on that skinny neck?" Pete asked.

Mama cried, "Pete!" but Albert only smiled.

"With invisible wires and a little magic." Albert winked at Mama and then pulled a quarter from behind Pete's ear.

Pete took the quarter. "Wow! I'd have to eat five worms to get this."

There were giggles all around.

"Speaking of worms," Albert said to me, "know how you can tell which end of a worm is which? Tickle it in the middle and see which end laughs!"

I groaned.

"Not my best, I agree." He grinned. "I do love me a good joke."

I raised one eyebrow. "I hope you find one."

He laughed and wiggled his ears.

When Edna was ready, Albert bowed to Mama, and they were off.

"I do hope she'll be all right," Mama said. "Albert may look funny, but he's kind and seems to care for Edna. I think he'll be good to her."

"Unless his head falls off," Pete said.

JANUARY 11, 1942
SUNDAY

"**Y**our pop may be late tonight, Millie, so you're in charge of dinner," Mama said. She put two cans of pork and beans on the counter. "Sorry. This is all we've got."

"Beans, beans, the musical fruit," Pete sang, stomping around the kitchen. *"The more you eat, the more you toot."*

"Peter Gordon McGonigle!" Mama shouted as she grabbed him by his shirt.

"He's all yours for a while, Mama," I said. "I'm going for a walk." I'd let Mama handle Pete and Lily and the house and everything until it was time for her to leave. I now knew she counted on me, but I was tired of being in charge while she worked. It was better when taking care of her family was Mama's job, not mine.

Pete had a tiny magnifying glass that he won in a box of Cracker Jacks once. I grabbed it and my book and set off.

I didn't see anything dead on the mudflats, so I took myself over to the ocean side. I squatted down but there were no dead things to look at there either, only sand. It didn't matter. The toy magnifying glass wasn't worth a hoot.

Icky Fribble and his fellow barbarians ran by, yelling and throwing sand and stones at some little kids on their bikes.

"Stop it, you juvenile delinquents," I shouted. "What's wrong with you?"

Icky stopped. "They're Japanese!" he said, throwing another stone at the fleeing children. "Enemies and probably spies."

"You dope. They're Chinese. My pop knows their father. He brings the kids along sometimes when he's delivering fish." What would Gram say? "And even if they were Japanese, they're little kids and Americans and not enemies."

"I think they're Japanese spies pretending to be Chinese." He looked at the magnifying glass in my hand. "Hmmm. A magnifying glass, Mil-bert? Very suspicious. Maybe you're a spy, too. Like your wacky cousin Edna. We ought to be stoning her, too. And you."

"Be serious."

"I am serious," Icky said. "I have to be on guard, being the man of the house now that Dwayne has joined the army."

"Which side?" I asked.

"Har-har, McGargle." Icky poised to launch a stone at me, so I took off.

I was walking, watching the waves tumble against the sand, when—

"Yeow! Damn! Son of a gun!"

Yelling? And swearing? There was someone down there by the water. The someone must have seen me, for he shouted out, "Hey, McGonigle! I need some help here!"

I went a little closer. It was Rocky, waving at me from the shallows. Dreamboat Rocky! And he was talking to me! He even knew my name! My heart fluttered like a humming-bird. I couldn't go any closer to him. I would trip. I would faint. I would die. Or worse.

Rocky waved again and shouted, "What in blazes are you doing? Come help me!"

I trudged through the sand to where Rocky lay on his side in the shallow water. Blood rushed from a gash on his leg, tinting the salt water pink.

"Stingray," he said. His leg was red and swollen, the gash deep and bleeding profusely.

My heart beat faster and my cheeks grew hot. It was like a dream—Rocky, lying there at my feet. I knelt and scooped water onto the cut with my hands to clean the sand off while Rocky thrashed and moaned. "Holy Toledo, that hurts!" he muttered.

"You need to see a doctor." My voice sounded squeaky and juvenile. Christopher Columbus! What was I, ten?

"No kidding, but first I need to get out of here, and I can't do it by myself." Rocky sucked in his breath. "Hurts like hell—uhh, heck. Sorry."

I tried to pull him to his feet, all the time thinking, *This is Rocky. I have his hands in mine. These are his muscles. This is Rocky and I am holding him.* Several times he got partway up and dropped back to the ground as I slipped and tripped.

Finally he was standing. Blood streamed from his wound as we stumbled back up to where the beach was dry. Rocky fell to the ground.

I took off my sweater and wrapped it around his leg to stanch the bleeding and tied the two arms to keep it tight. "What happened?"

"I was bodysurfing and landed on a stingray. Looks like he got me good."

I frowned at him. "You were just horsing around in the water? There's a war on, you know."

Rocky's face was pale and clammy. "I'm no soldier. I'm going to college. Be an engineer." His eyes filled with tears. "Why are we talking about this now? Quit yapping at me and get some help."

I stared at him. No longer a muscled dreamboat, a Greek god on a surfboard, he was just a boy, scared and in pain. He looked hardly older than Pete.

"Wait here," I told him. "I'll go get someone to help you." I plodded through the sand, tore up Ocean Front Walk, and left him behind.

Wait here? Where could he go with that gash in his leg? How stupid of me, but I didn't stop to think about it. I had Rocky to save.

I found Peter Palmer at the Burger Shack, and he went to pick Rocky up in the battered Plymouth he called the Surfmobile. I didn't go with him. I needed to think about Rocky. I felt a little disappointed. I wanted him to be a great hero, charging up hills and winning the war. But war was awful and people died. I didn't want Rocky to die. I imagined adding him to my Book of Dead Things and shuddered. Head spinning, I walked slowly home.

Lily was digging in the dirt in front of the cottage. She looked a bit pale. "Are you okay?" I asked her.

She nodded. "No wheezing." She poured dirt from a teapot into the bed of a dump truck. "But I wish Edna didn't live here. I don't like her."

"What has Edna ever done to you, besides stink up the house with perfume?"

"She said that sometimes fairies steal away a healthy baby and leave a sickly fairy child in its place. And that's what I am, she said. That's why I'm sick a lot. She told me not to tell Mama and Pop because they'd send me back. So don't you tell them."

Poor Lily. Her Shirley Temple curls were greasy and flat, her eyes deeply shadowed. She looked so worried and afraid. I clenched my teeth and frowned. Darn that Edna. I knew she was silly and confused sometimes, but I didn't know she could be mean. I, too, wished Edna didn't live here, but what could I do about it, except maybe get her drafted—and then watch out, U.S. Army!

"Applesauce!" I said to Lily. "I know it's really you and no fairy child." I pinched her chin. "I saw this dimple in your chin the day you were born, and it's still there."

"Really? Truly?"

"Would I lie to my favorite sister?"

Lily smiled and dumped dirt from the truck into teacups.

Lily would be okay, and Rocky would be okay, but what about me? My dreamboat had sunk.

JANUARY 14, 1942
WEDNESDAY

The sun was hot and the tide out. After school I went looking for dead things. I found a dead jellyfish and the carcass of a baby shark and squatted down to draw them in the book.

A voice from behind me said, "So that's what you do with that book you carry around—draw fish?" It was Rosie.

I hadn't yet told Rosie about the Book of Dead Things. It was between me and Gram. I wanted to tell her now, but what if she thought it creepy or babyish? I took a chance. "Dead fish and other dead things. And the names of people who died." I closed the book and tucked it into my pocket.

"Why dead things?"

"Well, for one thing, they don't move, so it's easier to draw them."

"Har-har, Millie. You do know that keeping a Book of Dead Things is weird? Even ghoulish and grisly," Rosie said.

"It's for my gram. She told me to keep track of dead people and things so I don't forget them."

"Do you really think she meant dead jellyfish and dog bones—yes, I heard about that."

I shrugged.

Rosie stared sideways at me. "No wonder you're gloomy a lot, Millie. You're allowed to have fun once in a while, you know, even during a war, even if your gram dies."

There was silence until Rosie added, "You know what you need, mournful Millie?" She grabbed my hand. "You need to jitterbug on the beach! C'mon, I'll teach you." She pulled me off the mudflats onto the sand. "Now relax and smile and do what I do."

She grabbed my left hand with her right hand, took my right hand in her left, and held them down toward our knees. "Now step back and close again. Swing out and swing in. Stick your butt out and swing, swing, swing!"

I stumbled and moved away.

"Hey, this is the easy part. Wait until we add flips and lifts and handstands." She danced by herself, butt out, fingers snapping.

"That looks pretty silly, Rosie." It did. And strange.

"Because we need music! Some Benny Goodman. *In the mood . . . dah dutton dah dah, doo wah doo wah . . .*"

"Still looks silly," I said, but not very loudly. I actually envied her style and her confidence.

Watching her closely, I began to lean over in a slouch, swivel my head, and flap my arms. It might not have been jitterbug exactly, but it felt good.

"Swing it, girls!" someone shouted. Gary Grayson and others were splashing through the water out past the mud.

"Hey, Rosie, you're cookin' with gas, lass!" called someone else.

Rosie waved, slouched down, and snapped her fingers.

"I dig that jive," Gary called. "We're going to get Cokes at the Shack and feed the jukebox. Wanna come with us?"

Rosie turned to me and raised her eyebrows in question.

"No, I've got homework."

"There's plenty of time."

"You go. Have fun. Fractions are calling me." I wanted to go, sort of, but—I don't know—it seemed so frivolous, especially with a Book of Dead Things in my pocket.

JANUARY 18, 1942
SUNDAY

After breakfast, while Pop was working, Mama slept, Edna and Lily and Pete engaged in a ferocious game of Go Fish, and the radio played the mournful and grim "Song of the Volga Boatmen"—*da da DA da*. After a commercial for the new Chevrolet Deluxe, a program started celebrating the life of the movie star Carole Lombard. She was *dead*! Why didn't I know that? She had died in a plane crash in Nevada two days ago as she was flying home from selling war bonds. I'd never seen her in a movie—Mama said I was too young—but the magazines I read at Bell's had stories and pictures about her romantic marriage to Clark Gable, who was the star of *Gone with the Wind*, which Mama let me see because it was historical, even though Clark Gable said *damn* in it, so her death seemed pretty personal.

"Go fish!" Pete hollered.

I jumped up and escaped outside. Mumbling angry words, I kicked pebbles all the way to the point and sat with my feet in the cold water. How could it happen? Carole

Lombard was young and beautiful and a movie star. If she could die, why not me? Or anyone?

And Clark Gable! How sad he must be. If only I could hold his hand and give it a sympathetic squeeze.

I'd have to write Carole Lombard in my Book of Dead Things. It had been a while since I'd added anyone's name. Probably I should also add soldiers and sailors who died in the war, but there were so many and I didn't know their names and it was becoming all too tragic and scary.

Both Mama and Rosie had called me gloomy, morbid, and peculiar. Was I? Did I enjoy all the sadness and worry like they said? But would it be dangerous to stop? I gnawed frantically at my thumbnail while tears dribbled down my cheeks. I wasn't crying for Carole Lombard and Clark Gable so much as for all the world, the dead and wounded, animals and people, the scared and angry and confused. I couldn't stand it.

A movement to my right turned out to be a large bird. A very large bird, as tall as Lily. I wiped my eyes and studied his blue-gray feathers and long, skinny brown legs. His face was nearly white, and a pair of plumes ran from just above his eye to the back of his head. It was a great blue heron standing ankle-deep in the water. I'd seen pictures but never a live one up so close.

I stood, startling the bird, who stared at me for a long moment before taking to the sky with slow, deep wingbeats, graceful and peaceful and so alive. I watched him fly, a large dark shape with legs trailing behind. Didn't some people believe in reincarnation? Carole Lombard had been on a plane that crashed. Could someone who died while flying now be a bird? Could that bird be Carole Lombard? And Gram—what kind of bird would she be? A chicken at the zoo? I smiled.

"Yo, Millie," I heard from behind me. Rosie. "Let's go for a walk."

"Absotively," I said. "But even better than a walk, we can swim to the Petersons' raft and stretch out in the sun. It's plenty warm and sunny still. What d'you say?"

The tide was high and small waves slapped against the shore. "Is it safe to go in there?" Rosie asked, scrunching up her nose.

"Sure. It's not like the ocean, no big waves or riptides. You just have to be careful not to step on a stingray or bump into a jellyfish. There are small leopard sharks sometimes, but they're more afraid of you than you are of them."

"I don't think that's true," said Rosie. Her face was kind of green.

"You're afraid? Aren't there fish in your lake?"

"Of course. Pike, perch, smallmouth bass. Nothing that stings or eats you. And I don't have to see or touch them."

"Okay, then," I said, "a walk it is."

We walked Dover Court over to the ocean side. Rosie started picking up stones and various bits and pieces from the sand. "What's this?" she asked, holding something up. "Why is it all smooth and frosty-looking?"

"It's sea glass, a piece of glass from broken bottles and such tumbled smooth by waves for years. Sometimes even a hundred years. I have lots of green pieces like that and some white ones, but no pink, purple, or red. They're awfully rare, but I'm still looking."

"This is a pretty piece," Rosie said, showing me a smooth, goldish glass shard.

"Rosie, beginner's luck! I've never found amber."

Rosie put the pieces in her pocket. "This might be my favorite thing about Mission Beach," she said. "Except for you."

We walked on. Waves were crashing on the beach and Rosie made sure she stayed far away. "Too big and dangerous for me."

I'd thought Rosie was braver and less jittery than me. She wasn't worried about bombs and war, being poor or dying, being embarrassed by Rocky. But she had fears, too— seagulls and the sea, stingrays and leopard sharks. Knowing that, I liked her even better.

There were no surfers out, but a bunch of boys were bodysurfing—swimming out past the breakers, catching and riding waves back to shore without a board. I tried it once but got sand and seawater up my nose, so I haven't tried it again. Yet. But maybe this summer.

When we got closer, I recognized Gary Grayson and Ralphie's big brother, Louie, in the water. Someone else stood in the surf but didn't go in any deeper. Someone with a bandage on his leg. Rocky. I turned aside, still not sure what to think about him.

"It's starting to cloud up," I told Rosie. "Let's go home."

JANUARY 24, 1942
SATURDAY

The Cap was sitting on the tumbledown porch of his shack as I approached. He was mending nets, holding them right up close to his eyes and squinting as he knotted.

"Can you still see to do that with your old eyes?" I asked him.

"Young McGonigle! Welcome. Don't you worry about me. I can see just fine up close. The rest is blurry but most of it I don't want to see anyway." He coughed a bubbly cough and spit over the porch railing. "How'd your abalone dive go?"

"Turns out you were right about it being too hard for me. At least I didn't get swept out to sea and came home with three perch in the bargain."

"Glad you're okay." He peered at me. "You know, you're growin' to look a bit like your gram."

Maybe, as soon as my hair turned red and I grew curvy. I liked the thought. "You knew my gram?"

"I shore did. She was a pistol, that Tillie."

He smiled but I could feel tears welling up. "I miss her

something terrible." I snuffled. "I still use the notebook she gave me to keep track of dead things and people."

The Cap frowned. "Doesn't sound like your gram. You sure that's what she wanted?"

I nodded. "I think so. She sort of said it would keep us safe. Like from the war." Cap said nothing, but he chewed on his mustache. "You fought in the Civil War, Cap. What was it like? Were you scared?"

He laughed a rumbling laugh. "Civil War? How old you think I am? I was in the Great War. 'The war to end war,' they called it." He spit over the rail again. "Landed here in 1920 and been here ever since. One thing I like about the beach is there ain't no war, no dead soldiers, no one shootin' at me." Cap shook his head. "I don't like talkin' about the war, and remembering the dead, and neither should you. You're a young thing, walkin' and breathin' and movin'. Don't get all strange and ghoulish."

"But I promised Gram—"

He waved me silent. "Horsefeathers! Your gram used to say we're too soon old and too long dead. She loved life and lived every minute. Last thing she'd want is for you to be all wrapped up with death and dead people."

I was confused. Was he right? Had I misunderstood her?

The Cap went on. "Mebbe instead of keeping company with dead things, you could do something to help fight against the evil that's come. That's what your gram would do." He rubbed his eyes. "Now I'm talked out. No more dark and gloomy. Go find something useful to do while you're young enough to do it."

I walked home slowly, my ears ringing with the captain's

words. I'd been so sure I knew what Gram meant, but did she truly want me all preoccupied with death and dead people? I wanted to think more about it, but Lily was waiting for me when I returned. "Will you put my hair in braids?"

"Why?"

"You know how I look like Shirley Temple?"

I nodded.

"Well, I don't want to look like Shirley Temple. I want to look like Lily McGonigle."

Well, I'll be a monkey's uncle. Good for her. I got a comb and ribbons and Gram's silver hairbrush—it seemed like a fitting occasion—and started brushing out Lily's curls.

"Ow ow ow!!!"

"Stop fidgeting, Lily. Don't be a pill."

I continued brushing, somewhat gentler. The rhythm was oddly soothing to both of us and there was quiet.

Into the silence Lily said, "You know when I got so sick last month? I'm sorry I didn't die."

I stopped brushing. "Why would you say that?"

"I know how you love dead things. You write their names and draw their pictures in your book. If I was dead, you'd love me and put me in your book, too."

I caught my breath. Did Lily really think I'd love her more if she were dead? She was a pill, but she was my sister. Didn't she know how scared I'd been when she was sick and how much I wanted her to live? Had I never told her? Or showed her? Apparently not. I'd just called her a pill and moved on.

As I plaited Lily's hair, I said, "Let me tell you a story." Lily stopped fidgeting to listen. "Once upon a time there was a girl who lived on an enchanted island with her little sister. The little sister was sometimes a pill and the older sister would lose her temper and be mean, but she loved her little sister. One day the fairies came and said they were there to whisk the little sister away to Fairyland because she was so good and they would leave an awful child in her place. 'Over my dead body,' said the older sister, and she grabbed the little girl. She hid her in the bread box behind the Wonder Bread, and when the fairies who were searching got too close, she moved her to the laundry basket. And when the fairies got too close to *that,* the older sister used her strength and her toughness to chase the fairies away. Finally they gave up and took another good child, leaving an awful child in its place, and that awful child is Icky Fribble."

"Yay! Icky!" Lily cried. "Millie, would you fight the fairies like that for me?"

"Of course, silly. That's why I told you the story."

"Yay!" said Lily again. She looked in the mirror at her new braids and said, "No more Shirley Temple!" and she lifted her arms and bent them as if to show off her muscles, if she had muscles.

The sight of pale, skinny Lily showing off her muscles was so funny I barked a sharp bark of laughter. It felt good, so I did it again.

No more Shirley Temple, I thought. That should be my motto, too. The captain was right. I was alive, so why was I still all involved with dead things and doing nothing useful? For Lily? For my family? For the war effort? I was getting sort of sick of dead things. Sometimes I forgot what the point was.

I brushed my own hair as I thought until electricity made it stand out from my head. My options, I knew, were a lot better than Rocky's or other young fellows'. No one was going to stick a rifle in my hand and send me out to shoot or be shot. I was perfectly safe. I'd been disappointed in Rocky for dodging his responsibility, but it wasn't my life on the line. And there were more ways to fight a war than picking up a gun.

I got up off my fanny and went to the Civilian Defense office on Mission Boulevard to see what I could find to do that didn't involve guns or bombs or being brave.

JANUARY 25, 1942
SUNDAY

After breakfast I sat at the table studying the material I'd gotten from Civilian Defense.

"What are those?" Pete asked, climbing onto my lap.

"Pamphlets."

"What are flamfuts?"

"*Pamphlets.* Booklets that tell about things that we can do to help fight the war."

"I thought the war would be done by now," Pete said.

"Not hardly."

"Then I want to fight the war, too."

"Good for you. Now pay attention. Since the war, the Japanese control all the rubber plantations in the world, so we can't get rubber. Stop wiggling! So the government is rationing tires and other rubber goods and asking people to turn in their old rubber, like tires, raincoats, hot-water bottles, bathing caps, girdles, garden hoses."

"Girdles," Pete giggled, swiveling his hips.

"Stop wiggling, I said."

"What does the government need girdles for?"

"They'll turn them into things the army needs."

"Like what?"

"I don't know. Tank tires."

"Tanks don't have tires."

"Forget it, Pete. Let the government figure out what to do with them. We'll just collect rubber things that people don't need anymore and turn them in. We'll need a wagon," I told him. "Do you think Ralphie will come with us so we can use his?" I hoped it had been well scrubbed since the dead-dog episode.

"Ralphie has chicken pops."

"*Pox.* Obviously then he won't be using the wagon. Let's go see if his mom will let us take it."

Pete jumped off my lap and we made our way across the back alley to Ralphie's house. Mrs. Rigoletto had a sign on their door.

"What's that say?" Pete asked.

"Official Fat-Collecting Station."

"Well, she hasn't collected much 'cuz she's the skinniest person I know."

I loved Pete! "I don't think she's collecting it on her body."

Mrs. Rigoletto opened the door. The whole house smelled like bacon. "We saw your sign," I told her. "What kind of fat do you collect and what's it for?"

Mrs. Rigoletto put her hands on her hips. *"Hello, Mrs. Rigoletto."*

"Hello, Mrs. Rigoletto," Pete and I chanted together.

"Hello, Millie, hello, Pete," said Mrs. Rigoletto.

"So what *do* you do with it?" Pete asked her.

"Cooking fats like bacon fat and meat drippings are used to make glycerin, and glycerin is used to make bombs."

"Bombs, wow!" said Pete. "Out of bacon fat. How do they do that?"

Mrs. Rigoletto shrugged. "I don't know. I just do my part by collecting it."

"That's what we want to do, too," I said. "Collect stuff to help with the war. I know Ralphie's sick, but can we maybe borrow his wagon?"

"Ralphie," his mother shouted. "Okay for Millie and Pete to use your wagon?"

"What for?" came Ralphie's shout back.

"War work," I hollered.

"Okay, but no dead dogs."

"Thanks, Ralphie. Hope you're better soon."

"The wagon's out in the carport," Mrs. Rigoletto said. "Be sure to come and tell Ralphie all about your day when he's not so contagious."

"Thanks, Mrs. Rigoletto," I said.

"Her house sure smells good," Pete said as we located the wagon. "Couldn't we maybe collect bacon rather than rubber?"

"Nope," I said.

We trundled the wagon up Bayside Walk. There was a blue star in the front window at the Fribbles'. So Icky was right. Dwayne had gone to war. Who would give the dreadful Dwayne a gun? Probably his fellow soldiers were in more danger from him than the enemy was.

I knocked and called for Rosie. I was hoping she'd want to help collect, but no one answered, so we started without her.

I trudged up to each door along Bayside Walk while Pete stood by the wagon. No one was home at the first three we tried.

"Jeepers, Millie," said Pete, flopping into the empty wagon, "this is no fun. I want to go home."

"Just wait. Someone's bound to be in and we'll get a wagonload of stuff to take to the collection center, and you'll be proud that you did your part to win the war."

At the very next place lived a lady so crotchety that I'd never even bothered to learn her name. I just called her the Great Grump. "Ahh, Grum—err, ma'am," I said when she answered the door, "we're collecting rubber for the war effort. Might you have any used rubber goods, such as hot-water bottles, bathing caps, or girdles, that you can donate?"

The lady snorted. "Girlie, if I had any of those things, I'd be using 'em myself. Now get off my property." And the door slammed. As I turned to go, I noticed the sign in the window: *Room for rent. No dogs, Jews, or Japs.*

Well, Gram, I thought, *the hate's the same as in your day. Just the names have changed.*

There were empty lots next and then Mr. Brundage's house. I went into my speech again, this time skipping talk of girdles and hot-water bottles, and asked instead, ". . . a rubber hose?"

"Hose? Look around you. Sand and mud. What use have I for a hose?"

Next door was the Grayson house. Nobody home. The

wagon was still empty. Didn't people in Mission Beach want to win the war? Pete and I went home for lunch and had egg-salad sandwiches with Lily that Mama had made before she left for work.

"I don't like knocking on doors and asking people for their old hot-water bottles and girdles," I said as we ate.

"Girdles," Pete giggled.

"Be serious. Let's see what else we could collect." I pulled the Civilian Defense pamphlet from my pocket. "How about tin cans? See here: *Collect, wash, and flatten. Prepare your cans for war!*"

"What will the army do with tin cans?" Lily asked.

"Tin's metal, isn't it, and they use metal for airplanes and tanks and stuff."

"Do you think Mama will make an airplane from the tin cans we find?"

"Could be."

Lily grinned. "Then I want to do it, too, collect cans."

"Think you can walk all the way? The wagon will be full of cans and there'll be no room for you."

"I've been wheezing less, and look, I got roses in my cheeks."

Her sunburn was long gone and she was pale but less pale than usual. "Okay, but no whining."

We hit the ocean side of Mission Beach, where there were more houses. And collecting cans proved much easier than scouting for girdles and hoses. Everyone had an empty can or two.

At Aldus Topper's filling station, Mr. Topper stuck his thumbs behind the bib of his overalls and said, "You kiddos are in luck. I been saving cans to take to the dump, but I never got round to it. Now you can have them."

We followed Mr. Topper behind the station. Slowly. Very slowly. Snails moved faster than Mr. Topper, I thought. Heck, rocks moved faster than Mr. Topper. Finally we reached a small mountain of motor-oil cans and even more beer cans. Mr. Topper gave us a big cardboard carton, which we filled with cans and loaded into the wagon. "Wait a minute, kiddos," he said, and he finished the beer he had been drinking and chucked that can, too, into the wagon, and I dragged it home.

The beer and motor-oil cans had no labels and were easily flattened, but the soup and tuna and Chef Boy-Ar-Dee cans had to be stripped of their labels and washed out first. "We'll need help," I told Lily and Pete.

"I'm too tired to do any more," Lily said, and she sat down on the walk.

"I'll get Artie and Archie and MeToo," Pete yelled as he tore off to find them.

The twins came to help but Artie said, "MeToo won't come. He's busy knitting and it's your fault, Millie."

"Hic," Archie added.

They began ripping off labels, but Artie cut himself on the jagged edge of a tomato-soup can and ran off for home, leaving a trail of drops on the ground that might have been blood or maybe tomato soup.

"I wanna see if he gets stitches," said Pete, and he, too, ran off, with Archie and Lily behind.

Christopher Columbus! The entire job fell to me. Finally the labels were off, and the cans were washed and flattened. I smelled like soup and beer and motor oil and had small cuts on my fingers. My arms hurt from pulling the wagon and my hands hurt from pulling labels and my feet hurt from stepping on cans. Trying to win the war was hard work.

After dinner, I pulled out a booklet I'd gotten from Riley Lenske at school: *Know Your War Planes.* It only cost me two cents because it was secondhand and had mustard stains on the cover. I'd been studying it for days and even failed a test at school on Friday because I was so busy learning planes that I forgot to study. Who cared about state capitals anyway in a war?

Enough junk collecting, I thought. *I'll be a plane spotter. Just sit comfortably and watch the sky. No more trudging around the beach with a wagon and junk for the war effort. No more beer and bean cans. Just looking at the sky.*

I lay on the sofa with my feet over the arm and drilled myself on Japanese planes until I could tell the Mitsubishi 97 "Sally" medium bomber from the Mitsubishi 01 "Betty" medium bomber. I learned the distinctive shapes of the Sasabo "Pete" seaplane and the Aichi 99 "Val" dive-bomber. Would German and Italian planes actually come as far as San Diego? Probably not, so I studied instead U.S. Army and Navy bombers: the Boeing B-17, the Douglas SBD, the Consolidated B-24, which Mama worked on, and so many, many more. It was, after all, a real war.

Finally I was ready to tackle Pop. He was home and in the kitchen, making school lunches for Monday. He had mastered bologna sandwiches, but his peanut butter and jelly still needed work.

"Pop," I said, scooping a fingerful of Skippy from the jar, "now that you have a job, can I have seven dollars?"

"Not likely. What do you need money for?"

"Binoculars. I want to be a plane spotter, so I'll need a telephone, binoculars, a pad of flash message forms, and an official identification book. I thought I'd start with the binoculars. The Sears catalog has good ones for seven dollars."

"Think again."

"But I've learned all about planes. Here, test me." I rattled off names and shapes until Pop called for mercy.

"Well, guess we should repay the five dollars you spent for Lily's doctor," he said. "I think I can find binoculars for five dollars at the Navy Exchange."

I hugged him quickly. "Thanks, Pop, and here's a tip for you: put the Skippy on the bread *before* the jelly. It'll spread better."

JANUARY 31, 1942
SATURDAY

"You sure read a lot," Rosie said as we walked to the library. "Do you want to be a teacher?"

I shook my head.

"A librarian?"

I shook my head again.

"I myself want to marry an explorer," she said, "and see some of those foreign places we hear about on the radio: Shanghai, Singapore, Java, Sumatra, Borneo, Hong Kong. They sound so exotic and mysterious. The war should be over when my time comes. How about you? What do you want to be?"

"Alive."

"Millie!"

"Really. I want to survive this war and have a normal life, right here on the bay. I'll have a bait barge in the summers for the fishermen and maybe repair fishing nets like Captain Charlie. I'm sure he'll show me how."

Rosie snorted. "I hope you're better at tying nets than knitting blanket squares for soldiers."

"Har-har, Rosie."

Rosie got herself a library card and I went to talk to Mrs. Pennyfeather.

She was behind the checkout counter. "Mrs. P, remember the last time I was here and I asked for sad and tragic books?"

Mrs. Pennyfeather raised one eyebrow. "I remember."

"Well, I don't seem to be in the mood today for depressing books about death. What do you have that's a little less sad? Not too happy but not tragic. Maybe even kind of fun. A little bit."

"You're in luck, Millie," she said. She pulled a book from a bookcase behind the desk. "I don't keep this out on the shelf because it is a little intense and violent at times for younger readers, but it should be just right for you."

The book jacket read *The Hobbit. The Hobbit?* What was a hobbit?

Mrs. Pennyfeather checked the book out and handed it to me. "Dwarves and elves, sorcerers and dragons, a quest and a battle. Some sadness, some death. Good against evil, much like today. I bet you'll like it."

Yowza! Dwarves and elves, sorcerers and dragons, a quest and a battle! I wished I could run right home to read, but I didn't want to desert Rosie. I should have, though. Everything else that happened that day was entirely her fault.

"Let's do it," Rosie said as we walked home. "Let's go to the USO dance tonight."

A group called the United Service Organizations, she told me, had places where sailors and soldiers could play games, eat cookies, and dance. Several of Dwayne Fribble's female friends said they were going to volunteer there. "We can make cookies and take them over and maybe have a dance or two. It must be so romantic, all those young men heading overseas to war, not knowing what their fate might be, and we'd be the last girls ever to dance with them." She gave a long, shuddering sigh.

Sometimes Rosie seemed much older than fourteen. Maybe girls grow up faster in big cities. Still, she was a friend, and I thought making cookies for sailors might comfort them and help the war effort. She could dance with them, and I could hear their stories about dead comrades and such.

"Okay," I said. "We'll have to bake at my house. Mama and Pop are going to visit Gram's grave, and Edna is out with Albert, so I have to stay home with the juveniles."

We entered the house as Mama and Pop left. "Mama and I used to make cookies together," I told Rosie. "We'll need flour, butter, and sugar. And eggs. But I don't think we have most of those things."

"Aunt Bertha keeps a supply of lard and molasses. Those should do. No eggs at the moment, but there's flour and . . . what else?"

"Cookies made of flour and lard don't sound very yummy." I searched through the cabinets in the kitchen. "Very old, very hard raisins? And Rice Krispies? At least they'd add some crunch."

"Sounds a little weird to me, but probably the sailors won't care," said Rosie.

I agreed.

"Great. I'll gather the molasses, flour, and lard from home and be right back." And she took off.

"We want to bake, too," said Lily, who peeped into the kitchen.

I gathered spoons and measuring cups, soap and water, some modeling clay, and a bowl of Rice Krispies and gave them to her. "Here. See what you guys can make out of that." Soon there were sounds of splashing and clattering from the bathroom.

When Rosie got back, we started mixing. Between the molasses and the Rice Krispies, the batter was a strange color and pretty lumpy. It didn't look anything like food, but I stirred it once more and dropped it by spoonfuls onto a baking sheet.

"How long should we bake them?" Rosie asked.

I shrugged. "I guess we'll just leave them in the oven until they crisp up."

Mama and Pop came home while we were still up to our elbows in splatters and spills and dirty dishes. "What's that awful smell?" Pop asked.

"We're baking cookies for servicemen," Rosie said. "I hope they taste better than they smell."

"Well," said Pop, wrinkling his nose, "I guess they'd have to."

Pop went out fishing on Mr. Conklin's new boat, and Mama closed herself in her bedroom to finish today's jingles. "It's hard to get inspired writing about drain cleaner and Northern Tissue splinter-free toilet paper. Still, a dollar is a dollar." She was working now, but I guess old money worries still stuck around.

I took the cookie sheet out of the oven. The cookies— or rather cookie, for all the batter had run together to make one giant cookie—were definitely crispy. Even hard. And burned.

I tried cutting it into neat squares, but no knife could cut through, so we just broke it into bits. They'd taste just as good that way. Or that was what I imagined, because I wasn't about to taste any of the odd-looking things.

Lily and Pete popped up. "Can we have some?"

"Okay. Here's one for you, Pete." He grabbed it and stuffed it in his mouth and tried to chew. "And you, Lily."

After a few attempts to eat the cookies, they spit them out in the sink. I should have known better than to slip a kid a bad cookie. They stared at me with such a look of betrayal, as if I had killed some soft fuzzy animal or something. Good gravy. Let the sailors have the awful things.

I emptied out my school bag and put the cookies in. "The USO is all the way downtown, Rosie. We don't have bus fare, and it'll be dark in a couple of hours."

"Oh, Millie, grow up. I have plenty of nickels for the fare, and we'll be back long before it's dark."

"Well, Mama's here now, so she can take over kiddie duty. They're her kids." I called, "Mama, Rosie and I are taking the cookies to the USO." But not very loud in case she said no.

"Millie, you can't go downtown in torn shorts and bare feet," Rosie said. "We have to look like young ladies appropriate for cheering up the troops." I pulled on a skirt and my school shoes. Wearing shoes on a Saturday. How awful. I hoped it would be worth it.

The bus dropped us off on Broadway. I'd never seen downtown so congested. The streets were jammed with buses and trolleys, and the sidewalks were a sea of blue capped with little white hats. We passed bars, restaurants, tattoo parlors, and pool halls so packed with people they were spilling out onto the street. There was a busy bowling alley, a penny arcade, and shops crowded with all sorts of dumb souvenirs, like fringed U.S. Navy pillows, San Diego Mission tablecloths, and men's shirts with bright green palm trees. The movie theater was playing *Sergeant York* with Gary Cooper. You couldn't even get away from the war at the movies.

The USO was on the second floor of a building near Dr. Cowan, Credit Dentist. "I don't hear any dancing," Rosie said as we walked up the stairs. But someone was playing a piano and plenty of people were talking and laughing.

A tall woman in a flowered dress and tightly curled hair met us at the door at the top. She seemed friendly enough until you looked into her eyes. Smart and sharp. There'd be no getting around her. "Can I help you, girls?"

"Not at all," said Rosie. "We've come to help *you*. We brought cookies we baked to cheer up our brave fighting men, and we thought we might stay for a dance or two—"

"The dances are held at the ballroom at the amusement center," the woman said. "We do have junior volunteers here who talk and play cards with the servicemen, but they're all over eighteen."

"Umm, so are we," said Rosie, standing tall. "And we have cookies." She opened the bag and pulled out a shard of cookie.

"I appreciate your willingness to help," the woman said, looking at the cookie like it was a dead fish. I could tell she was trying not to laugh. It was totally humiliating. "Come back in four or five years. And take my advice: use the time to practice making cookies." She closed the door, shutting us out.

"Four or five years?" Rosie wailed. "The war will probably be over by then and we'll miss all the fun. I hate being too young."

Fun? Was she kidding? I didn't think there was much about the war that was fun. I dumped the cookie bits into a trash receptacle on the corner. They probably would have poisoned our brave fighting men anyway. I should have thrown the school bag in with it. It would never lose that burned-cookie smell. But I had to admit that life was a lot more interesting with Rosie around. Even the peculiar parts.

When I got home, I was in the doghouse. If we had two doghouses, I'd be in both of them. Lily and Pete had helped themselves to the leftover flour and molasses we'd abandoned in the kitchen. The bathroom looked like there had been an explosion in a gingerbread factory.

Mama had gone to work at the aircraft plant, but Pop bawled me out for leaving the mess in the kitchen and sent me to clean it up, and the bathroom, too. I had to go to bed without supper but I didn't really mind. Dinner was Brussels sprouts and perch.

FEBRUARY 4, 1942
WEDNESDAY

My school was having a newspaper collection drive. Apparently we needed more paper to win the war. After school I thought I'd borrow Ralphie's wagon, but on the way I ran into Ralphie's brother Louie out collecting with it. Suddenly everyone was helping to win the war. "Dicky Fribble has a wagon you might borrow," Louie said.

I'd see us lose the war before I asked Icky for a favor, but if Rosie were around and *she* borrowed it, she and I could work together.

There was no one home at the Fribbles'. Where was Rosie? The day felt a little empty without her. Wagonless, I retired from newspaper collecting and headed for home. On my way, I wrote a **McGONIGLE** in the mud. There was a small sand shark dead in the shallows, but I had forgotten to bring my book. I threw the little shark back into the water.

I watched the sky all the way home, on the lookout for enemy planes. I saw several American planes—mostly

Liberator heavy bombers and Coronado and Catalina patrol bombers—but, to my relief, not one Japanese Mitsubishi bomber. I didn't write **MCGONIGLE** in the sand. Too much trouble.

At home, I flopped on my bed and picked up *The Hobbit* where I'd left off. The hero is Bilbo Baggins, a small and humanlike being with hairy feet, called a hobbit. He and lots of creatures—other hobbits, dwarves, elves, heroic eagles, and a wizard—join together to battle evil trolls and rescue a treasure from Smaug the dragon. Smaug is mean and violent and evil, and the creatures unite to fight him. Mrs. P was right—the story was kind of like today, but more fun.

Mama came home then from shopping and I helped her put away groceries. "You can't believe how much things cost these days," she said. "Prices are going up and up. Why, I had to pay eight cents for a loaf of bread that was seven cents only last month, and twenty-four cents for a pound of coffee, not to mention six cents a pound for sugar, but there isn't any to buy. Even with our jobs, we may be reduced to eating pickleweed and sand! Thank goodness your pop fishes."

I could see from the groceries what we'd be eating: whatever was relatively cheap—macaroni, oranges, cabbage, carrots, corn flakes, tomato soup, prunes, chicken necks and backs for soup. Hooray, there were peanut butter and Swiss cheese! But no meat, no cake, no Hershey bars.

"I saw Bertha Fribble at the market," Mama said. "She squeaked on and on in that air-raid-siren voice of hers, something about Rosie not helping her, eating too much, and going downtown looking for sailors. And using up all her lard and molasses. 'Good thing my butter, sugar, and eggs are safely hidden away,' Bertha said. Which means she's hoarding."

"What about Icky? He's more trouble than Rosie could ever be."

"I didn't ask her. My ears were hurting me already. Anyway, the upshot is that Bertha kicked Rosie out, so Rosie and her mother went back to Chicago."

I swear my heart stopped. "Rosie's gone? You mean it? That's true?"

"That's what Bertha said. Lillian and Rosie caught a train on Sunday."

"Is she coming back? Did she leave me a note? Say anything? Anything?"

Mama just shook her head, saying, "I'm sorry, I don't know."

I stormed out of the house and kicked everything I could kick. The side of the house. Driftwood, pickleweed, eelgrass clumps. Rosie gone! I thought we were friends. It was just how Gram left, without any warning, leaving me alone.

I was sitting outside feeling bitter and forlorn when Pop came over. "Your mama has gone to work," he said. "I brought home hot dogs and marshmallows, and I say we need a bonfire."

"Pop, it's too cold."

"That's why we need a bonfire."

"Please don't say it will cheer me up. I'll never be cheery again."

Pop built the fire with newspapers and driftwood. It flickered at first and then grew bright and leaping in the dusk. I lay facing west so I could see the oranges and pinks and violets in the sunset sky.

"I've figured out a way to get rich," Pete said with his mouth full. "Louie Rigoletto said there will soon be a shortage of gumballs because gum is made from sugar and some rubbery stuff from trees where the war is. Anyway, I now have six bubble-gum balls. I'm hoping to trade them for a chemistry set or a wagon."

"If you can find someone who'll give you a wagon for only six gumballs," I said.

"Gumballs are worth a lot of money now. Three cents each. I traded a pair of my corduroys and a sweater to get these six—"

"You traded your clothes for eighteen cents' worth of gum? What's wrong with you?" Pop rubbed the back of his neck and sighed. "Go and get your clothes back. And no more trading."

"I don't like long pants and sweaters anyway."

"Pete!"

"Okay, okay. Phooey. I wanted to trade Lily's doll but no one would take it."

Lily squealed. "Don't you touch Pancake or I'll—"

More squabbles. "I'm taking a walk."

"Can I come?" Lily and Pete both asked.

"No, you squirts stay here with me," Pop said. "I think Millie needs some time on her own."

I walked away, over to the ocean side, where waves were

crashing. I splashed through the water. My chest tightened and squeezed, and my head filled with tears. Was I mourning for Rosie? For Gram? Or for me?

Walking home, I passed the Fribbles'. No Rosie there now. Could life be any worse?

FEBRUARY 8, 1942
SUNDAY

We were still finishing our breakfast CheeriOats when Mama hustled into the kitchen. "Hurry, hurry, my little ducklings! We're off to save the zoo!"

Lily and Pete shouted, "Yay! Hooray!" but I asked, "What? How? When?"

"Because of the war," Mama said, drinking Pop's cold leftover coffee, "zoo attendance is down. I'm afraid if people don't go, the city will close it or make it into another naval hospital, so hurry, ducks, we're going to the zoo." She yawned.

I hadn't seen Mama up so early since she started on the night shift. She must really care about saving the zoo. Or maybe she was just more relaxed and less worried now that she was working at a real job. As usual I felt funny about playing and having fun during wartime, but gee whiz, I was only twelve and couldn't be gloomy all the time. I thought of what I'd said to Rocky. It was unfair, I guess. Let him surf sometimes and I'll go to the zoo.

"Lily, you look nice," Mama said, but she frowned at my shorts. "Millie, go put on a dress and some shoes."

Holy cow. A dress? Shoes? Were we going to the zoo or to meet the queen? "But, Mama—"

"You too, Pete."

He snorted. "A dress?"

"Shoes, Pete."

Mrs. Fribble was at the bus stop when we got there. "Lois," she shrieked to Mama, "are you going to Japantown to hunt for bargains, too?"

"I didn't know you shopped there," Mama said. "I hear their produce is the best and—"

"Shop?" Another shriek. "From the Japanese? I would never! The devils would likely poison you." She climbed aboard the bus, followed by Mama and us kids. There were no seats, so we all stood in the aisle, stumbling and swaying. "There's talk that all Japanese people may be forced to move away from the West Coast, so they're packing up and going before that happens."

She smiled, but she looked to me like the Wicked Witch of the West in the *Wizard of Oz* movie. I fully expected her to turn green and snarl, *"I'll get you, my pretty, and your little dog, too!"*

"There's all sorts of things they can't carry with them," Mrs. Fribble continued. "Pianos and refrigerators, toasters and radios and kitchen supplies. We real Americans deserve to have them after what the Japs did to Pearl Harbor. I myself am in search of a painted china tea set. And anything silver. Real silver."

I saw Mama's brow furrow and her eyes narrow. "Don't

they have enough trouble without people circling them like sharks, ready to pick off their belongings?" she asked Mrs. Fribble. "They're not criminals. The Japanese of San Diego weren't anywhere near Pearl Harbor."

"Come on, Lois. You know they're all in it. They're spies and saboteurs, every one." She leaned in closer. "Here in California we're sitting ducks for enemy subs. I've seen them myself, huge, dark shapes cruising offshore."

Mama's eyes grew narrower still as Mrs. Fribble went on. "The government tries to tell us they're whales! Bah! Who can trust the dictator Roosevelt and his commie pals. Vernon and I are thinking of moving away from the coast to Arizona, but there are so many Mexicans there."

Mama's face was grim and her eyes were mere slits, but I could see a glimmer of angry green. "Bertha Fribble," Mama growled, "you infuriate me. You're a bigot, small-minded and intolerant. You should be ashamed of such vile opinions!" I thought Mama would explode. Other people on the bus looked away or started mumbling to each other. Mrs. Fribble said nothing but pulled the cord for her stop. I waved to her as she departed. "*Adios,* Mrs. Fribble. Enjoy Arizona."

Pete and Lily each clutched one of my hands. Their faces looked stunned. Mama shouting?

Mama looked at the three of us and sighed, clapping a hand to her chest. Her cheeks flushed pink. "My babies, I'm so sorry. I shouldn't have lost my temper and scared you. But I couldn't let her get away with spouting that garbage without speaking up."

Mama reminded me of someone. Who? Someone who marched for justice and stood up for people who needed it and . . . Of course. I smiled. "No, Mama, you were right. You're a hero, just like Gram, even if you were a little loud."

"Hero?" Mama smiled. "As this war goes on, you may hear that sort of thinking more and more. I hope you handle it better than I did."

No, Mama, you did good. Could I be as brave?

The bus turned toward Balboa Park and drove close to Consolidated Aircraft, where Mama worked. I pressed my nose to the window, excited to see, if only from the road, the place that built a B-24 Liberator bomber every three hours.

Odd shadows flickered through the window. High above, the road was covered over with cloth. "What's that for, Mama?" Lily asked.

"That's camouflage netting they've hung over downtown, the aircraft plant, and the airport. The nets are painted to look like trees and streets and houses from above to fool enemy aircraft."

"You mean enemy planes are coming here?" asked Pete.

"With bombs?" Lily asked, and her lip trembled.

"Don't worry. If they do come," said Mama, "we'll fool them with our camouflage nets. There are even fake trees and false house roofs on top. And see those?" she continued, pointing to huge balloons that looked like blimps on steel cables. "They're called barrage balloons and are meant to scare low-flying enemy aircraft and tangle them in the cables. There are more than a hundred of them up there, here and at the airport and the park."

I chewed a few fingernails. Enemy planes flying over San Diego? Would that mean war right here? Could balloons really save us? Shaking my head, I wondered about the common sense of the people in charge. Balloons?

Most of Balboa Park was closed and turned into hospitals for sailors. A few museums and, best of all, the zoo were still open. Children were always free at the zoo, but Mama had to pay twenty-five cents.

"I thought you might think the zoo a frill," I said.

"Not today," said Mama as she took Lily's hand. "Besides, now that Pop and I are both working, we can afford an occasional frill."

I'll have to remember that she said that, I thought. *It will come in handy.*

Once we were inside, the familiar smells and sounds of the zoo lifted my heart. So many memories of Gram and the animals. There were a number of men in navy uniforms, a few soldiers, and flocks of chickens, pecking at the ground, the grass, and my feet. They must miss Gram coming every day to feed them. I would.

"Chickens!" Pete yelled. He put his fists in his armpits and flapped, crowing, *"Yankee Doodle-doo!"*

"Well, Pete," I said, "the volume was impressive, but it's *roosters* who crow, not chickens, and it's *cock*-a-doodle-doo. You should probably know that at five and a half."

"I'm not five and a half," Pete said. "I'm almost six."

"Hey, I guess you are." He was. The last half year had been full of changes and challenges—the war, Mama and Pop going to work, Rosie coming and going, Gram dying. 1942 was only one-twelfth over. What would the rest of the year bring? And in the summer I'd turn thirteen. I'd be a teen! Christopher Columbus, what would *that* be like?

"What should we see first?" Mama asked as she gathered us around her.

"Gorillas! Elephants! Giraffes!" we shouted, all at the same time, and we ran down the walkways, up onto the mesas, and into the canyons. We visited Mbongo and Ngagi, the gorillas, first. They were enormous, like giant hairy babies, rolling and wrestling and making strange gorilla noises.

"They look a bit like Dwayne and Icky Fribble," I said.

Lily stared at them a minute. "No, the gorillas are cuter."

"I'll bet they weigh a million pounds," said Pete.

"Each," said Lily.

"I think that one wants to shake my hand," Pete said as he tried to squeeze his hand through the bars of the cage.

"Pete, no petting the wild animals," Mama said, pulling him away. "Or should I say, the *other* wild animals."

Pete growled and she patted his head. "Down, boy," she said.

We pointed at the camels, laughed at the seals, and wondered at the size of the elephants. At the wire bird–of–prey enclosure on Primate Mesa, Pete said he was a vulture and climbed up the side. Lily squeaked and squealed at the newborn ocelot kittens, and I pretended I didn't know either one of them.

Finally we were all tired and nearly as dusty as the animals. While Mama and Pete ran ahead to use the bathrooms, Lily took my hand and we said goodbye to the monkeys. "Look at those funny ones with red faces, Millie." She pointed and laughed. "They look sunburned. Like I was."

Apparently she had forgiven me for the sunburn. I read

the sign that identified the monkeys. "Those are Japanese macaques, also called snow monkeys."

Lily squeezed my hand tighter. "Japanese? Are they bad, like Mrs. Fribble said the Japanese are, even in San Diego?"

There was something in the trusting way Lily looked at me, as if I had all the answers, that touched my heart. I squeezed her hand. "Don't listen to Mrs. Fribble. I know she's a grown-up, but she's wrong about so many things and she hates a lot of people. Listen to Mama." *And Gram,* I said to myself.

We walked back to the bus stop through Balboa Park. Barrage balloons floated above us. If they'd been red and yellow, it would have looked like a giant's birthday party. Despite their ominous intent, I smiled at that. Jiminy Cricket, I was actually having fun.

I finished *The Hobbit* after dinner. If Mrs. P lets me renew it, I'll start reading it all over again, it's that good. It was so thrilling and exciting with heroes and battles, horrible villains, a wonderful wizard, that awful dragon, and the pitiful, small and slimy and totally creepy Sméagol, who wants to kill and eat Bilbo. There were scary parts, sad parts, funny parts, and parts that made me cheer.

I loved Bilbo, who was reluctant and fearful at first, but by facing dangers and his fears, he gets more confident and wise and sort of grows up. Could that be why Mrs. P suggested the book to me?

FEBRUARY 15, 1942
SUNDAY

I'd been confused as to time all week since President Roosevelt declared year-round Daylight Saving Time, to be called War Time, and had us turn our clocks ahead. I guess it gave people an extra hour of daylight in the evening, but it sure made it hard for people—well, me—to get out of bed in the morning. And how could a man, even a president, just change time? Could he also say, *From now on February is May, so the weather will be warmer*? I didn't get it.

Edna must have been out early, and she still wasn't back when Mama left for work. Mama had a double shift today, so when she got home, she'd likely need a double sleep. We wouldn't be seeing her for a while. Pop was at the Navy Exchange. Pete and Lily had been playing outside, but the door flew open with a bang.

"Millie, look, Millie," Pete cried. "I lost a tooth." And sure enough, one of his bottom front teeth was missing. No, not missing. Just not in his mouth. In his hand. "Look, here it is. Isn't it terrific?" He held it aloft. "I'm a big boy now!"

Big and getting bigger. He ran back out to show the rest of

Mission Beach his terrific tooth. I'd miss this gap-toothed wise guy with his little-boy smell and big grin when he was all grown up.

I walked over to the Fribbles' to see if they knew anything about Rosie. I sure missed her. I couldn't think of anything worse than having and then losing a friend.

There was no one home, but a gold star hung in the front window. Not blue. Gold. My face froze. It meant Dwayne Fribble had died in the war.

Lots of soldiers died, of course, but Dwayne was someone I knew, someone only seventeen. And he was permanently gone. I'd never see him goofing off and being a nuisance again. There obviously were worse things than Rosie leaving. Shame on me.

I felt sorry for being so flip about wanting to add him to my Book of Dead Things last year. I didn't know he would really die. *Goodbye, Dwayne,* I thought. *You were a pain and a thug, but I didn't wish you dead.* I wondered how Mrs. Fribble was managing. She was probably the only one who loved and mourned the dreadful Dwayne.

I thought I should write a few preventive **MCGONIGLE**s in the mud, but I didn't feel like it. This had been happening lately. Too much on my mind, I supposed. I headed home.

Edna was there. I followed the trail of gardenia perfume into the bedroom and dropped onto the bed. Edna had a funny sort of smile on her face as she pulled things out of the dresser drawers and stuffed them into a carryall. What wouldn't fit—perfumes and creams, old *Photoplay* magazines, her scuffed slippers—went into a grocery bag.

"What's up?" I asked her.

"I'm leaving. Albert and I just got married."

I jumped to my feet. "What??"

"Married. Albert made all the arrangements. He's good at arrangements."

"But you'll be Mrs. Wizzleskerkifizzlewitz!"

"I'll get used to it."

"Does Mama know? Is this okay with her?"

"It's my decision, not your mama's," Edna said. "Albert is good to me. He wanted to marry me, and I couldn't think of a reason not to."

I took a pink brassiere from Edna's bag and held it up to my chest. Nope, still some time before I needed one. "Do you love him?"

Edna grabbed back her bra. "I'm tired of living in other people's houses. I want my own house, my own rules." She chewed on her lip. "I forget things and mix things up, but Albert doesn't mind that I have a screw loose. He says that's why I need him." The edges of her mouth began to turn up a little.

"What about the war? Won't he be drafted?"

"His family has a farm up near Bakersfield. He said people who grow food are too important to the U.S. to be drafted." She looked in the mirror and patted her hair. "I'll get me a straw hat and be a farmerette."

"Why didn't you invite us to the wedding? Lily and I could have been flower girls."

"Phooey. It's wartime. No time for frilly weddings." She closed her empty drawer with a slam. "Now help me find my glasses."

I found them. "Edna, they're on top of your head."

She patted her head. "So they are." She looked around the room. "I'm almost ready. When Albert gets here, we'll drive right on up to Bakersfield. Maybe have a wedding supper at the counter at Woolworth's on the way."

It didn't sound very romantic to me, but then Edna and Albert were pretty old. I couldn't imagine what Mama would think of it all.

Pete and Lily came home hungry. I was cutting apple slices and Velveeta cheese for a quick lunch when Albert came to fetch Edna. Pete bounded over to him, but Lily hid herself behind me.

Albert took off his hat. "Hiya, kids," he said. "How's things?"

"Fine. We're all fine," I told him. "Edna says she'll be ready in a minute."

"Good, then I'll have time to try the beach jokes I've been working on for you." He cleared his throat, tightened his tie, and said, "It's a good day. I just drove past the ocean, and it waved at me."

I grinned and Lily giggled behind her fingers, but Pete just shrugged.

"Not funny, Pete? Well, then, how about this one. Why can't you starve on the beach? Because of the *sand which* is there."

Pete shrugged again. "Mostly I don't get jokes. Will you pull a quarter from my ear again?"

"Ears don't always have quarters in them, you know." Albert took his handkerchief and sneezed loudly. "But lookee here, I managed to sneeze out a quarter." I thought it pretty gross, but a laughing Pete snatched the quarter from the handkerchief.

Lily, coming out from behind me, whispered, "And me?"

"Well, little lady, do you want a joke or a quarter?"

"Both."

"I can tell you live near the ocean," Albert said, "because of your *wavy* hair." He reached out and pulled a quarter from the curls escaping from Lily's braids. She squeaked again but smiled.

I wished I were young enough to have quarters in my hair—I could use some spending money.

"I guess you kids hate to see Edna go," Albert said.

I pinched Pete's arm before he could answer and said, "Though I look forward to having my bed back, of course we'll miss her." *But not,* I said to myself, *the overpowering scent of Jungle Gardenia.*

"So long, kids," Edna said as she entered, pinning her best hat on her head. "Don't feel too sad to see me go. I've sprinkled perfume inside the dresser drawers to remind you of me."

Yikes! I'd be washing everything in that dresser as soon as I could. Can one fit a dresser in a washing machine?

Albert patted Lily and Pete on their heads, shook my hand, and left a quarter in my palm. He picked up Edna's bags and hurried out. Edna gave each of us a quick gardenia-scented hug and followed him out. "Tell your mama and pop thanks for me and goodbye," she said, and with that she was gone.

"I'm so happy to see Edna leave," Lily said. "She won't be telling me scary fairy stories anymore."

"Me too," I said. "I get my bed back. Let's have a celebration dance." I turned on the radio, looking for music, and Lily started twirling and swaying.

Instead of music, I found news headlines: *"The Battle of Singapore has ended in a decisive Japanese victory. All Allied military forces were forced to surrender unconditionally. Prime Minister Winston Churchill called it 'the worst disaster in British military history.'"*

Lily stopped dancing. Her shoulders slumped and her lower lip trembled. "Is the celebration over? Do you have to go and write their names in your dead book now, Millie?"

Holy cow, now I'd gotten Lily disappointed, gloomy, and worried. She thought I liked dead things more than living things. And Pete had brought me a dead dog! How many more people would I infect with my morbid preoccupation? Lily and Pete were too young and alive to have to be involved with dreadful, sad things like I did.

Or did I? Oh, Gram, I wish you were here to talk to. Tears prickled my eyes. *Why did you give me the book and then leave?*

It was the middle of the night when I woke and heard Mama come in. Wrapped up in my blanket like a corn dog, I pattered into the kitchen and found her pouring a cup of coffee.

"Millie, what are you doing up?"

"I have to tell you about Edna." So I did.

"I hope she'll be okay," Mama said as she slurped. "Albert told me he had been thinking about asking her to marry him for a while, but he was worried she wouldn't want to leave us." She poured another cup of coffee. Two whole cups. We must be rich.

"Are you sad that she's gone?"

Mama shook her head with a smile. "No. I'm a little concerned, but life will be easier for us without her. Albert will care for her and she won't be too far away." She snuffled. "I just hope this would be okay with my mama."

And suddenly Gram was right there in the room with us, beaming like a little light. It was okay that Edna left, I thought she was saying. She wanted us all to be happy. Happy. Of course she did. I took Mama's hand.

FEBRUARY 22, 1942
SUNDAY

In the early morning I was out by the bay skipping stones, hoping to clear my head. It had rained a little in the night, so the air was clean and crisp, and the shadow of a crescent moon still hung in the sky. I kicked through the sand, singing my rain song. Most people sang, "Rain, rain, go away," but I wrote mine this way: "Rain, rain, won't you stay? And come again any day."

The song didn't work. It never does. The sun came out and began to warm the beach, so more and more folks turned up to enjoy it. Some kids were splashing through the shallows followed by a woman, her frothy gray hair dancing in the sea breeze. A small girl in a pink sweater called to her, "C'mon, Granny. Play with us."

The grandma said, "You kids go have fun. Have a good time. I'll watch you."

I remembered the many times Gram with her big laugh and her sunburned nose had joined us on the beach. I felt heavy with missing her. "Go have fun," she'd say, just like this grandma. "Have a good time."

I headed to the south end of Mission Beach, to the channel where the peaceful bay became ocean and the ocean filled the bay. Walking carefully on the rocks, I went out to the end of the jetty, where the channel was deep and dangerous. I was not on land anymore but almost standing in the ocean, feeling its power. It was a good place for thinking.

And I needed to think. I was more and more confused about Gram's book idea. If she wanted me to have fun and be happy, why did she urge me to keep track of dead things? Is that truly what she wanted? The Book of Dead Things—that wasn't even Gram's title. It was mine.

A cool wind rose and drove me off the jetty and back to the bay. The beach was lively. A bunch of kids were playing baseball. Someone flew a kite. A swarm of seagulls had found the remains of an abandoned lunch and were attacking it and each other, screeching like a whole army of Mrs. Fribbles.

I plopped down on the beach. I picked up a sand dollar and sat still for a minute, examining its soft and sandy surface. It weighed very little and was starting to smell, so I knew it was dead—but newly dead, for its velvety bristles were a soft purple, not yet dry and bleached. I hadn't ever seen one so almost alive.

"What's that?" asked a small voice. It was the little girl in the pink sweater.

"It's a sand dollar. A kind of flat sea urchin."

"It's pretty."

"It's dead."

"I don't care. It's pretty." She took it and examined it closely before handing it back to me and running to her family.

I studied the sand dollar. There was a flowerlike pattern

embossed on its top side that was the violet you sometimes see in the sky at sunset. On the underside was the tracing of a star. The little girl was right. It *was* pretty. That's what she'd remember. Not that it was dead, but that it was pretty.

Could that be what Gram wanted me to do? Not to collect dead things just because they were dead but to notice and remember what was good or pretty or meaningful even if it was gone? The sand dollar. Pete's terrific tooth. Rosie's nose all white and shiny with zinc oxide. Rocky and his board in the sunshine.

I held my breath, then jumped up and splashed frantically through the shallows before flinging the sand dollar deep into the bay. My chest grew tight and my thoughts swirled around my head like smoke from Pop's pipe.

Whatever is lost stays alive if we remember it, Gram had said. Of course. How could I have thought she meant I should draw dead crabs and make lists of dead people?

Oh, Gram, I miss you. But a spot of something—anger, maybe—still hung on. How could Gram have left me to carry on without her? It was partly her fault I misread her. Wasn't it?

I knew she didn't choose to leave me. It was like Pete blaming the Lone Ranger for dying. And that spot in me that might have been anger eased a bit.

Gram was alive in my heart and my memory, but she was dead for real. The image of her in a box in the ground made the sadness in my chest swell like her Irish soda bread rising. Death was real. The war was real. People dying was real. Florence and Rosie were gone for real. So much loss. My eyes stung. I had a heavy load of mourning to do.

And I had plenty of tears for all of them: for Gram, for dead soldiers and sailors and all the others killed by bombs and guns all over the world, for the little girl with the floppy bunny, for the poor dead sea creatures I found on the beach, and the pitiful dead dog who was once loved by someone.

I wailed, shedding enough tears to fill another bay. I stomped and kicked, threw stones into the water, and a dead jellyfish and a live crab. If I'd had my book with me, I'd have thrown it in, too. The book that I thought would please my gram, keep me safe, keep the war away.

The tears eventually dried up. I took a deep breath and let it out slowly. I thought I finally understood why Gram suggested the book, but I'd had enough. No more. I was done with the Book of Dead Things. What should I do to finish it? Not just throw it away. A ceremony was called for, but what? Burial on the beach? Burial at sea? A bonfire?

I remembered what Skippy Morrison had said about Viking funerals. "That's the ticket!" I shouted to the gulls. I'd fold the book's pages into little paper boats, set fire to them, and sail them out to sea, like Skippy said the Vikings did to honor their dead. Or at least out into the bay. It seemed a grand plan, exotic, elegant, full of drama, and definitely final. I hurried home to start.

Mama had gone to work but she left me a dollar bill and a grocery list for Bell's, which was open every day now. Mr. Bell said it was his way of serving our fighting men. I was to get two cans of Chef Boy-Ar-Dee spaghetti, bread, milk, oranges, and eggs. *You may keep the change,* she wrote. Yes! I'd be a careful shopper to make sure there was change.

I left Bell's, tucking a dime into my pocket, just as an

old woman leaning on a cane was leaving. I held the door open for her. "You're Mrs. Dunsmore, aren't you? I'm Millie McGonigle. You know my mama."

"Yes, the nice woman and the curly-haired little girl. Tell them I enjoyed the casserole and the brownies. Especially the brownies."

"How's your broken leg?"

"Mending," she said, shifting her cane and a bag of groceries from one arm to the other. "Mending slowly, but mending."

We walked together from Mission Boulevard to Bayside Walk, where she'd head north and I south. Her grocery bag changed arms again and again, and she slouched over, panting, her face red from effort.

I shifted my own bags. "Mrs. D, let me carry that home for you."

"No. I need to do this, dear. To move, tough it out, push myself to live like a person and not an old broken thing." She lifted her chin and set her jaw.

She wouldn't let me have the grocery bag, but I walked with her a way to make sure she was okay before I turned back for home. She sure was stubborn. And brave. A kind of hero. Not just soldiers in the war were heroes but also this very old woman with a broken leg who refused to lie down and die.

I was putting the groceries away when Pop came home to take Pete for a haircut and a hamburger bribe. Pete hated haircuts but Pop said, "You look like Prince Valiant from the comics, which is not a good look for a five-and-a-half-year-old boy."

"Almost six" was the last I heard as Pop took Pete's hand and they headed for the barber's.

I made tuna sandwiches with the crusts cut off and warm watery tea. "Come on, Lily. We're going to have a tea party like in *Alice in Wonderland*."

"Can my doll Butterscotch come?"

"Of course. It wouldn't be a party without her." We sat at the table and I poured Lily's tea. "Now listen, I've decided that I'll no longer have a Book of Dead Things. It's too mournful and I don't want it anymore."

Lily nodded solemnly but curiously.

"Help me tear out the pages," I said, "and we'll send them away to sea." I felt a twinge as I saw the lists of dead people and the sea-creature drawings pile up, but I decided my ceremony would be a way of honoring all of them. Then I could let them go. I showed Lily how to fold paper boats like Gram had taught me. I smiled. *I love you, Gram,* I thought.

I took a box of matches from the kitchen drawer. Good thing Mama was at work and Pop and Pete weren't home yet. They'd have kittens at the thought of their girls and fire. If I was old enough to take charge of Lily and Pete and take them marching to Mission Boulevard and fish for food for dinner, I thought, I was old enough to do this.

"We should be dressed for a celebration," I said, so Lily and I draped ourselves in scarves and ribbons and shared Mama's bangle bracelets between us. We waved our arms and jingled our bracelets and twirled our scarves. "We are"—I remembered a spelling word—"resplendent!"

"Respend it!" Lily crowed.

"Exactly," I said.

Then, with our boats in a grocery bag, we hurried over to the point to launch them.

The first few matches blew out before getting near the boats. "Well, crumb, where did this breeze come from?" I lifted the boats out of the water and waited for calm. Finally, with their paper sails on fire, we sent the boats bobbing in the gently lapping water.

As we watched them drift, I twirled and chanted, *"I send my fears to the sea. They'll no longer trouble me. No more worry, no more dread. Millie and Lily like living instead!"*

Lily laughed and said, "That's as good as Mama's jingles." She danced and twirled, shouting, *"No more dead. Living instead!"*

"Lily, you're a poet, too!"

She grinned at the praise. Such a little thing from me made her so happy.

The burning boats crumpled softly into the water. I exhaled deeply. To my surprise, I started to laugh. Christopher Columbus! All that time and all that effort and it was a mistake, a gigantic misunderstanding! I felt foolish and embarrassed but also relieved. Light. Alive. Even hopeful. Joe Btfsplk would have to live under his rain cloud all by himself.

I gave the boats a last salute and grabbed Lily's hand, and we ran home.

On the way I noticed little purple flowers on the pickleweed, a hermit crab struggling to carry his house on his back, and a piece of sea glass, round and smooth and blue as the sky. I could have drawn such lovely things in my old book instead of dead shrimp.

But I did enjoy looking closely at the dead creatures I

drew, examining them, studying them, finding what was odd or funny or mysterious about them. I'd miss that.

Maybe, I thought as Lily and I shuffled through the sand, maybe I should start a new book, with drawings of living things, like moon jellies and starfish and sagewort, and people to celebrate and cherish: lovable people like Lily and Pete and Rosie. Brave people like Dwayne Fribble, who went to war and died there—and maybe even Rocky, who braved the criticism of his decision not to go. And Mrs. Dunsmore, who chooses life.

Yes, a new book, a book of life, My Book of Life. I'd be sure to include a drawing of the pretty purple sand dollar, Lily's new blond braids, and Pete's funny, freckled, almost-six face. And I just happened to have ten cents for a new notebook. I'd think it a good omen, if I believed in omens. It was good luck anyway.

That night I told Lily, "I'm going to start a new book, a book of life, full of beautiful, wonderful things that I love, and Miss Lily's picture will be on page one!"

"Me, Millie? You love me?"

"Of course. I just didn't notice for a while." I hugged her, and I meant it.

"I decided on my doll's forever name," she said. "It's Millie Junior."

"That's sweet, Lily, but let's see what you think tomorrow."

"She'll still be Millie Junior tomorrow, and that's final. Millie Junior and I voted on it."

Mama was awake early the next morning. She made herself a cup of coffee and I had Ovaltine. Not hot chocolate, which had gone to war, but warm and sweet. Mama and Pop both working had sure improved our menu. Maybe soon a lamb chop or a roast chicken would find us.

"I heard from Lily," she said, "that you were playing with matches last night, setting things on fire. Do I need to worry about you when I'm at work?"

I smiled. "Not playing exactly, Mama. We had a ceremony, I was very careful, and I won't have to do it again." I spread grape jelly on my toast and took a bite. I realized I had never told Mama or Pop about the Book of Dead Things. They wouldn't have approved and maybe would have stopped me. At the very least I'd have gotten a cheer-up lecture. "The ceremony was pretty silly but it felt important. I was working on something in my notebook but I was finished. It had to go, but not just into the trash. I needed something big and dramatic and, oh, final."

Mama put her arm around my shoulders. "My Millie, my interesting, original, wonderfully odd Millie. What would I do without you to brighten my day?"

Brighten? Old doom-and-gloom Millie? What was happening? I leaned into Mama's warm side, careful not to get jelly on her bathrobe.

FEBRUARY 28, 1942
SATURDAY

Rosie wrote me a letter! She didn't move back to Chicago for good but only until her family packs up and moves west! The warm beach weather was good for her mother's lungs, so the whole family will be living here permanently.

> *We left so fast I didn't have time to tell you. We've rented a house at the north end of Mission Beach, close by the Piggly Wiggly and just over a mile from you. My dad, who's too old for the army, will join a law firm there and my mom will get better. We move in June and next year you and I will be at Pacific Beach Junior High together! Luckily my brother will have graduated to tormenting the high school. Leo is almost as bad as Icky but much cuter, and girls seem to like him. Explain that. Can I bring you anything from Chicago?*

You, I thought. *I miss you.* But instead I wrote and said, *How about a picture postcard of your Lake Michigan? Does it look like Mission Bay?*

Pop had a day off, so he treated Lily and Pete to a picnic lunch at the point while Mama slept off her double shift. I stayed home to finish my letter and took it to the post office to mail.

The day was sunny and warm with a soft breeze. Perfect spring weather. The curlews, sandpipers, plovers, and oyster-catchers would be leaving us for the summer, to be replaced by flocks of tourists. Travel posters at the market and the library and the window of the real-estate office on Mission Boulevard lured visitors with the promise of San Diego sunshine but also offered *the sight of big ships slipping in and out of the harbor, squadrons of planes crossing the sky, and aircraft searchlights sweeping the night.* I shivered. Did people really come to San Diego to see signs of war? Creepy.

The war was changing the world, and I didn't know if it could be changed back. But there will always be the same sky, the same ocean, the same bay. There will be the tides flowing in and out, the fishy smell of the mudflats, the squawks of the gulls, the peace of the small waves on the bay, and the sparkle of the sun on the quiet blue water. I took a slow, deep breath.

But what about me? Was I the same person I was before the war started? I didn't think so. The war came like an earthquake and shook everything and everybody up, and I, like the world, was changing.

I crossed over to Mission Boulevard and put the letter in the drop box at the post office. Mission was no longer crowded with soldiers and sailors and marines. The war had taken them away, and they were off fighting other soldiers somewhere. But there was Spider Grossman. No aloha shirt. No swim trunks. This Spider was a soldier.

"You in a uniform?" I asked. "I thought you joined nothing."

Spider saluted. "Uncle Sam called me."

"San Diego's a navy town. Why didn't you join the navy?"

"I've seen enough anchor tattoos to last me a lifetime. No way. Just call me Private Grossman, U.S. Army."

"What'll happen to your tattoo parlor?"

"Why? You wanting a tattoo?" I grimaced, and Spider snickered. "My brother's still here, inking anchors and *Mom* tattoos while I'll be on a tropical island in the South Pacific, under a coconut palm, drinking cocktails with rum and fruit." He patted his army duffel. "I even packed an aloha shirt, just in case." He saluted again as he left, duffel over his shoulder.

I hope you're only joking, Private Grossman. I knew enough from the radio about the dangers of the army in the South Pacific. I shook my head as I crossed over to the ocean side.

The beach was packed with barefoot girls in bathing suits, sunburned women and children, and old folks with their faces to the sky, but very few young men.

I had spent ten cents from Albert's quarter to buy a war-bond stamp at school. I calculated that only 187 more dimes would entitle me to buy a twenty-five-dollar bond and help win the war. I'd used three cents for the stamp to mail my letter to Rosie and saved two cents toward a bottle of nail polish for my newly grown fingernails, even though Mama wouldn't let me wear it until high school. The final ten cents would buy me a cheeseburger at the Burger Shack. The Shack, I heard, had a new person behind the counter. A tall person with wavy hair and a smile like a toothpaste ad.

Rocky. Would my heart pound and my hands grow sweaty like they used to?

Rocky took a wet rag and wiped the counter in front of me. Did he remember me?

"How's your leg?" I asked him. "Did it heal okay? Can you still surf?"

"Yeah, I'm fine, but I don't have much time for surfing. I start college in June." He put a stack of napkins down. "I know you don't think much of me, skipping the service to go to school, but the country needs engineers, too, you know."

So he did remember.

"Sorry, Rocky. I was bossy and wrong. I shouldn't have judged you," I said. "If you want to fight the war by being an engineer instead of a soldier, do it. I'm sure you'll be a fine engineer." Rocky smiled, and my face grew hot. He was still a dreamboat. That hadn't changed. I wiped my sweaty hands on my shorts.

Rocky gave me the burger and slipped me a Pepsi on the house. The mustard tingled my tongue, and grease rolled down my chin. You can't beat a Burger Shack burger.

As I crossed back to the bay, I passed Mr. Bell sitting on a bench in front of his store, sunning his shiny white shins. "Well, lookee here, it's the McGonigle girl. Out enjoying the spring sunshine?"

"I think the new year should start in spring. Everything is new and fresh and hopeful." I sat down next to him. "It's weird. The war brought big changes to the rest of the world, but Mission Beach seems mostly the same."

"Well," said Mr. Bell, "some changes are just harder to

see. My son Walter is a fighter pilot over Germany, and Simon, my youngest, is in the navy, too. We don't know exactly where he is." His eyes grew teary for a minute before he went on. "Sugar is hard to get, there's no butter and very little meat to sell, and I'm blamed for the shortages. I think sometimes about catching octopus and selling it as steak." He shook his head.

"You could go into business with George."

"Haven't seen George in a while. The navy ordered the Portuguese tuna boats to work as supply and patrol boats in the Pacific. George joined his brother on his boat." Mr. Bell smiled. "They're officially the Yacht Patrol, but because they deliver food, everyone calls them the Pork Chop Express. Wish they'd express a few of those pork chops this way."

"I think of George sometimes, with his squirt bottle of bleach," I said. "I thought it was so sad that the octopuses were yanked out of their comfortable dens just to be killed and eaten."

"The war has yanked many of us out of our comfortable dens, but not all change is bad. With no boys at home to fuss over, Mrs. Bell is happily volunteering with the Red Cross. My brothers-in-law have fine new jobs at Consolidated Aircraft, and I myself have made new friends while scouring San Diego for groceries. And you look prettier than ever." He winked.

"You're a smoothie, Mr. Bell." I waved goodbye and headed down San Gabriel to the bay. The sound of the gulls, the smell of the mud, and the softly lapping water just offshore were my world, my home, familiar and soothing. My shoulders relaxed as I inhaled and exhaled slowly and deeply. I took off my shoes and wrote a big **MCGONIGLE** in the mud before it was gone.

Then I added an exclamation point—**MCGONIGLE!** This time it was not for protection but celebration. After months of bad war news, the radio reported that the U.S. Navy was gaining in the Pacific. No one said the war would be over soon, but any good news was long overdue and welcome. Lily was less sickly, she still got A's in arithmetic, and her doll was still named Millie Junior. Pete was wheeling and dealing his way into bubble-gum riches without trading away his clothes. Rosie was coming back and we would be together in junior high in the fall. I would be a teenager at last. Mama and Pop were happy to be working and doing their bit for the war effort. I could see in their faces the uncertainty that change brought but also the possibilities. Did my face look like that, too? I hoped so. I wrote in the mud once more: **MILLIE! MILLIE MCGONIGLE!** And I grinned.

On Bayside Walk, Pete, Ralphie, and MeToo were pulling Ralphie's wagon, loaded with metal parts that clanked and clunked. "Good for you guys," I said with a salute. "I can see the movie now: *Pete, Ralphie, and MeToo Win the War!*"

"Me too!" shouted MeToo.

Icky came barreling down the walk on his bicycle, tooting his horn. I was feeling different these days. Lighter and even cheery. I didn't need an archenemy. Could we be friends? Should I stop telling him to drop dead? Should I lie and say something nice about Dwayne? Just in case, I gave Icky a small smile.

He swerved so close to me that I had to jump off the walk. "If it ain't Mil-dreadful, ugly as ever," he called as he passed by.

I shrugged. Some things, I thought, never change.

AUTHOR'S NOTE

On December 7, 1941, war came to America's children. Some picked up toy guns and shot at pretend enemies. Others had nightmares for the rest of their lives. Millie thought the war came like an earthquake and shook everything and everybody up. The terrible years of the Great Depression, with poverty and unemployment, soup kitchens and shantytowns, were ending.

War brought new opportunities—women went to work at aircraft and munitions factories. Millions of men of all creeds and colors could join the armed forces. The government built thousands and thousands of houses across the country for workers and families.

But the war also brought troubles: sacrifice and dislocation, new fears, a new enemy, the internment of Japanese Americans, air-raid drills, food shortages, and constant war news on the new and scary radio. I wondered how a young person, after suffering through the deprivations of the Depression, coped with the upheaval. I knew she'd need to find courage and solace somewhere.

For many years I'd heard my husband Philip's stories about their small house on the bay, long before the bay was dredged and Mission Bay became a famous resort. The warm bay water lapped at the sand when the tide was in. There was swimming and surfing, and children went without shoes from June until September, and their feet grew callused and summer-wide.

Phil would row his small boat out where the reeds and cordgrass grew tall and read comic books until his nose was sunburned and his empty stomach growled. He watched seals tumble in the water and fished for perch and halibut, although more often his hook brought up stingrays and little sharks, which flopped in the bottom of the leaky boat.

Most intriguing to me were descriptions of the vast mud-flats, stinking, slippery, and mysterious, which appeared like magic when the tide was out. The mud was pocked with pickleweed and eelgrass. Shoals and small islands, home to colonies of mussels and to sand dollars that stood on end in soldier-like rows, were revealed. The mudflats teemed with insects and small crustaceans, which drew curlews, sandpipers, and plovers, who poked in the mud for their dinner. And early in the morning, Portuguese fishermen would be out catching the octopuses, whose hiding holes the ebbing tide had uncovered.

I knew I wanted this for anxious, fearful, worried Millie. As the world changed, Millie could find strength and wisdom through simple things and the natural world, nurtured and soothed by the tides flowing in and out, the fishy smell of the mudflats, the squawks of the gulls, the peace of the small